A ROMP WITH A ROGUE

LORDS OF TEMPTATION

LORDS OF SCANDAL SPINOFF

TAMMY ANDRESEN

Keep up with all the latest news, sales, freebies, and releases by joining my newsletter!

www.tammyandresen.com

Hugs!

CHAPTER ONE

MISS ABIGAIL WENTWORTH sat as still as still could be as she waited for the tirade to end. She cocked her head thoughtfully to the side, clasping her hands together in her lap as her cousin went on and on...

What was Clarence on about again?

She tried to remember the thread, hoping her eyes hadn't glazed in a way that would alert him she wasn't listening. He didn't like it when she stopped listening.

The story had been long and dull, not that one could tell from his level of agitation.

Quietly, she remembered the thread of his words. The tale about a man who had slighted him at his club that afternoon.

Now that she thought about it, she distinctly remembered a few lines. They played back in her mind as she continued her pretense of listening and glancing about the second-floor drawing room. The room was unchanged from her childhood, soft pink silk curtains, cream pillows, highly polished wood. But everything felt different now. Cast in a darker light.

"And then he'd informed me that I was not welcome at his table. Can you believe that?"

Yes. Yes, she could.

But she shook her head sympathetically, molding her features in a show of solace.

"I'm the new baron," he railed. "How dare that bastard say such a thing to me?" His hand flew up in the air as she forced herself to focus.

The first time Clarence had gone on such a tirade, she'd been frightened out of her wits. He grew so animated, his face turning purple, his arms waving wildly. And when she'd asked a probing question about what he'd done to provoke such negative behavior from another, *wham.* The back of his hand had come down across her cheek so hard and so fast, stars had exploded behind her eyes.

Even now, her fingers came up to stroke the skin along her cheekbone, which had been bruised for weeks.

She'd been shocked and appalled that first time. What great offense had she committed that warranted such treatment? But no answer had become apparent.

So she'd learned…

Better to make sympathetic noises, say as little as possible. Give him the appearance of attendance while letting her mind drift far away.

The problem was not in her method, it was sound. The issue now was how often she was forced to keep up this façade—almost daily. And how many more times she'd need to in the future.

Clarence was her distant cousin and heir to her father's title. When her father had passed five months prior, Clarence had been on a tour of France and it had taken some time to bring him back.

But now that he was here, he was inescapable. In her present…but in her future as well.

Clarence had decided that he and Abigail should marry. The new Baron Westphal wanted her as his baroness. And she was in no position to deny him. It was impossible.

This was going to be her life.

Her shoulders, held rigidly straight, began to curve forward at the thought as she attempted to hide the grief that always overwhelmed her at the idea of marrying her cousin.

"He said I was sniveling drivel and that he'd had more masculine rags with which to clean his boots."

The words filtered into her thoughts. She tended to agree with whomever Clarence's unnamed aggressor had been. But instead, she just made some outraged noise deep in her throat, tiredness pulling her shoulders down even further.

She knew better than to allow her exhaustion to show. Her shoulders should be set in indignation. He turned toward her and stopped, his gaze narrowing.

"Abigail," his words cut through her, the sharp, dark tone of them, making her shoulders snap straight again.

"Yes, my lord?" she asked, fear sliding down her spine as she swallowed the lump that had risen in her throat.

He might be short and thin but that didn't mean he didn't have a wiry strength that outmatched her in every regard.

She'd been subject to a sharp hit from him on more than one occasion and she knew enough to do everything in her power to avoid being hit again.

"Why do you look like that?" His lip curled in distaste. "Do I bore you?"

She shook her head, thinking quickly. "I am frustrated on your behalf, my lord. That is all."

He gave a slow nod and then he reached out and lightly patted her shoulder. "Of course, my dear. That does make sense."

Abby swallowed again. She might not respect Clarence Westphal, a spoiled, lazy man who thought the world owed him every advantage, but she respected his backhand. Her father had never hit her; he hadn't been the most affectionate or loving man, but he'd not openly abused her, she could say that.

But Clarence had no such qualms. She twisted her gloved fingers together as she drew in a shuddering breath. There was nothing to do but allow him to rail out all his malice. "What else happened?"

Clarence returned to pacing. "Let me see. He..." His lip curled again as he paused. "Was some dark-haired, hulking, untamed beast of a man who clearly grew up without a shred of refinement. He must have inherited his position, because he surely wasn't born into it."

Her brows rose. Clarence was tossing that barb? Not that she agreed with him. A man's worth was in his actions, not his birth, but why Clarence would think the other man less for not having been born the son of a lord was a complete mystery to her. But she kept her mouth closed, lips pressed tightly together.

"And he just oozed this rough masculinity like sap from a tree. He had his feet on the chair across from him. Can you believe that? At White's."

She had no idea how men behaved in their clubs away from the eyes of women, but Clarence clearly wasn't thinking that particular detail through as he tossed out the insult.

And she doubted many of the lords she knew would ever do something so crass as put their shoes on nice furniture. Not even at a gentlemen's club. "I can't."

"And he had this grin. Like he saw right through me." Clarence stabbed at the air, his bony fingers jerking with his movements. Only a few years her senior, Clarence appeared much older than the two and twenty she knew him to be. "But I see through him. He's an uncouth animal."

She nipped at her lip. Had he said who...who this man was? The one who had so clearly gotten under Clarence's skin?

She wished she knew. She'd like to send him a basket filled with fruit or pastries. Not that she'd ever be allowed to do such a thing. But perhaps at some point she could give her thanks. Show her regard to the man who'd said all the words she could not. He had effortlessly hurled all the words at Clarence that sat bitter on her tongue daily.

Clarence deserved each and every one of them, just as he deserved the irritation coursing through him now.

Not that it was difficult to rile Clarence. He was forever obsessing about various slights. But still. Clarence was upset, even for him.

Did she dare ask the name of the man? Had he spoken the identity of the offender when she'd stopped paying attention? If he had, he'd be terribly angry if she posed the question.

So she didn't want to ask.

Still, she'd like to know the person who so directly and easily dug under Clarence's skin. At the very least, she'd like to shake his hand.

That last thought made her smile and she ducked her chin quickly to hide the curve of her lips. Imagine if she could find another man who could put Clarence in his place. The sort of man who might be her hero.

A soft sigh escaped her lips. What a lovely dream.

———

LORD RUSHTON SMITH, Rush to everyone who knew him well, sat in his carriage and chuckled. He hadn't been this amused in weeks.

Actually, he couldn't remember the last time he'd felt this…light.

Not since his family had purchased the gaming hell, Hell's Corner. And even before that, the weight of financial strain, and the burden of supporting his family, had been oppressive. He raked his fingers through his hair and sat back in his seat.

This was why a man should just work with his hands. It was steady. Even. He'd always found his hands to be his most consistent tool.

They'd hoped the club would provide them with a dependable income. And it had been a financial boon, there was no denying that. But it had tied him even more tightly to his family, and this life in London, at a time when he wished to escape. And Hell's Corner created one problem after another.

There was the man who wished to purchase the gaming hell from them, which sounded like a solution, though the offer had been anything but. When his eldest brother had refused the offer, the solicitor had attacked Rush's sister, Mirabelle. They still weren't sure about the perpetrator's true name or who he worked for, but he was a danger lurking in the background that had hardly allowed Rush rest.

While he no longer wished to be beholden to his family, he'd not leave them in a crisis. Rush had found a new job, one he was very excited about. He'd become the estate manager for a merchant who'd purchased a large estate west of London. The position would utilize his accounting skills, but he'd also spend a fair bit of time on the grounds, outdoors where he belonged.

Best of all, his new boss spent most of his time in London, so Rush would be there without an overseer most of the time. A position that suited him.

And it was time for him to gain some autonomy from his family. His brothers each had a life independent of the club, of their siblings, but for him… Every action he took was for the betterment of his brothers and sisters. And it was choking him.

One might have thought that running an illegal gaming hell was perfect for a man who'd been raised on the East End of London. He'd grown up amongst criminals and thieves.

But Rush wanted more than just to live in the shadows of the seedy underbelly. He wished to move and think and breathe. Besides —since when did running a criminal operation mean he was chained to a desk, turning as soft as his waste of a father? It cut him to think of himself as just another worker bee growing weak in an operation that didn't suit him at all. None of his brothers had to chafe under such restraint. The tension in him had been building for weeks.

But today…today he'd had a bit of fun and it had been so satisfying.

Some tiny and pompous man had strutted into White's, calling out his importance and his position and how everyone ought to take note of him.

Rush did. He noted thinning hair, weak arms, pasty skin, as though he rarely stepped outdoors. A gut and a chin that belied his thin frame. The man was everything he hated about the peerage: weak, sniveling, and yet full of his own pompous worth. It was like a disease among them.

He was the opposite man to Rush in every way. Though to be fair, of late, he'd also spent a great deal of his time indoors, calculating numbers. He was the only one of his brothers who was any good at the endeavor, even if he still preferred to be physical. He'd much rather be swinging an axe, riding a horse, or wrestling a man.

What did that make him exactly? His whole life he'd been a man without a country. He didn't belong anywhere. He wasn't a gentleman despite the title of *Lord*, nor was he a laborer as his muscles implied. He didn't fit with his brothers, nor his father, the peerage, or the working class. He was a man without purpose, a ship without a rudder or a port, and it made him itch to strike out and find his own place in the world.

One that valued the thickness of his chest, the bulk of his biceps, and the power in his thighs as much as it did his business sense.

But he digressed. The little weasel had come in, loudly bloviating on his position, and then he'd stopped in front of Rush's table. His beady eyes had homed in on Rush's feet, placed in another chair, and that weasel's gaze had managed to narrow.

How eyes that small worked their way smaller still, Rush couldn't say, but they did. The other man's lip had curled and then the little rat had demanded that Rush make room for a baron.

He might not belong in the world of lords, but he'd not bow or scrape to it. Never.

Rush might have told him that he was the heir apparent to a marquessate. But honestly, the position was so new, he'd completely forgotten and if he were honest, he didn't hold much value in a position of the peerage. A man's actions should measure his worth, not the title given to him by his father. And if superiority were measured by blood, why was he, as a bastard son, less? Shouldn't he be as important as a baron?

Honestly, he didn't understand the system enough to know if the baron outranked him. Rush's father had been an earl and he'd tried to teach all his sons the class system, but as bastards, they'd just assumed they'd find their lives and livelihoods outside of the drawing rooms of London, so Rush had never much paid attention.

So when the man had challenged him, Rush had responded the way he knew how, with aggression.

He had not hit the man. Even he had his limits.

But he'd let the little shit know that he didn't bow to weasels or barons. Period.

The beady-eyed little weasel had gone off in such a huff that Rush had been filled with satisfaction since.

Perhaps he needed to recommence boxing sessions with his brother Tris, who boxed professionally and would surely beat the dickens out of Rush, but even that would feel good. He needed to sharpen up with a fight. Needed to loosen his muscles and his mind with hard physical activity. He'd lost it these last months and a good beating always reprioritized his thinking.

He had a plan of where he wished to go and what he wanted to do, but he'd yet to decide how to extricate himself from his family. They needed him now. His new boss had been kind enough to delay Rush's start, but Rush would have to find a way out soon...

Ace, their eldest brother, had removed their sisters from London, leaving only him and his brothers behind. And without the girls to smooth the brothers' rough edges, tempers in the house had been running high. One more reason he'd have to be careful how he made his exit.

Fulton had been on a run to Italy to move another shipment of wine, but he, Tris, and Gris had been circling each other like lions in a cage.

That was surely why he'd not fulfilled his sister Mirabelle's request to check on her little friend who'd gotten herself a nasty guardian.

He pulled the bit of parchment out of his coat, the one with the chit's name and address. Lady Abigail Wentworth. He frowned.

Rush had only met her once, but he already knew she was far too beautiful to be the sort of woman he protected. His attraction to her had been instant, sizzling through his veins like fire on kindling. A man couldn't guard a lady like that and not get...ideas.

Hell, he'd already had them. Something about her fragile beauty called to him and he didn't like it.

And that was the last thing he needed, to confuse his place in this world further. There were a few truths he understood absolutely. He wasn't the marrying kind, he was the dregs. A rough-and-tumble warrior.

And his father's lack of attention had proved something else too.

He'd never be part of the elite world. If even his earl of a father didn't love him, why would any member of the peerage?

Which meant he was never to touch her. Her beauty was to be admired at a great distance and not more closely.

But he'd promised Mirabelle, and he was currently relaxed thanks to his modest victory—and so today he'd go see Abigail.

And then he'd call this duty fulfilled.

Once and for all. He could write to Mirabelle and explain that Abigail was fine. That the new guardian was good enough and that all this worry was just women being women.

He had two sisters, after all. Meddling was like breathing to them. Necessary.

The carriage rolled up to an elegant-looking townhouse, and some of his good mood evaporated as he scowled at the stately brick-front home.

See? She lived in luxury. What would she have to complain about?

He stepped out of the carriage and bounded up the steps two at a time, then rapped with the knocker.

A butler answered the door with a frown. "Yes?"

"Lord Smith," he said. Even he knew that he wasn't supposed to ask for an audience with an unmarried woman without invitation. But he didn't know her guardian's name.

For a brief moment, the butler's gaze clouded with confusion before he opened the door wider. "I'll get Baron Westphal."

Westphal? The name niggled in his gut, sounding uncomfortably familiar.

Westphal? Wasn't that the name of the man who'd…

But he didn't finish his thought, because appearing at the top of the stairs was the little weasel. Well, didn't that just fucking figure.

CHAPTER TWO

"WHAT ARE YOU DOING HERE?"

Abby could practically hear the spit flying from Clarence's mouth as he spoke from the hall.

She froze. Did she step out? Stay put? He sounded angry. The sort of angry that she carefully attempted to avoid.

"It's you," a deep baritone called back. The sound of the other man's voice shivered through her, both richly masculine and oddly familiar.

Without meaning to, she rose from her seat, twisting her hands as she craned to catch a glimpse of him. But from her spot in the sitting room, she could see no further than the banister and not down into the foyer. Not from here.

Who was the man who'd so immediately upset Clarence? Curiosity and dread settled in her stomach as she drew in a trembling breath.

"What are you doing in my house?" Clarence snarled, tension making his back stiff and straight.

"Your house? Is this not the home of Lady Abigail?"

"What business do *you* have with her?" Clarence's voice sounded tight and hard, a sure sign the anger was rising.

But the other man didn't seem to care. "That is none of your concern."

Her breath caught in her chest as Clarence spun to her, his face twisted and angry. "He's here to see you."

It wasn't a statement. No, the words were an accusation, as vicious and cutting as the mean look pulling at the corners of his eyes. She froze. "I don't even know who you mean."

But then the man with that deep baritone came into view, striding up the stairs, and she gasped in a breath. She'd recognize Mirabelle's brother anywhere. Lord Smith.

Tall and devastatingly handsome in that dark and mysterious way, with near-black, wavy hair and deep, dark, glittering eyes, he had the sort of lean cheekbones and a sharp jaw that might make a woman swoon if she weren't in such danger. The only thing that softened his face at all was the fullness of his lips.

His neck was thick and corded, with his cravat off and his shirt open to expose the sun-kissed skin. His shoulders were broad, tapering down to narrow hips and powerful thighs. He trotted up the stairs as though he put in no effort at all.

So entranced with the man before her, she'd forgotten all about Clarence until he was next to her. She started in surprise, her heart thrumming in her ears as she tried to breathe. But fear was pounding through her limbs as Clarence's face twisted in rage.

She had the presence of mind to take a step back before his claw-like hand clamped over her upper arm, dragging her closer.

How could a man that thin be that strong? Was she just that weak? But she couldn't ask as Clarence leaned close to her face. "How do you know this miscreant, Abigail? Tell me now!"

She drew in a shuddering breath, her gaze meeting Lord Smith's as her jaw opened and closed again. "Please, my lord. He is the brother of the Marquess of Highgrove."

"Highgrove?" Clarence spat. "I should have known." He released her arm to turn back to Smith. "But just as you did not allow me to sit at your table, you are not allowed in my home and you are certainly not allowed to consort with my wife-to-be."

"Your wife-to-be?" Lord Smith said loudly, standing up straighter as his chest seemed to expand. His gaze settled on her as he skimmed her length. "I can see why Mirabelle was concerned."

"Mirabelle?" Clarence, quicker than a snake, grasped her arm again before he gave her a violent shake. "You know how I hate surprises." She attempted not to cry out in pain but he held her so tightly, she was certain to bruise. Her teeth snapped together as she attempted to gain some ground with which to move away.

"I know." Clarence did not like anything unexpected. He was only satisfied with complete control. Had no one ever told him no? His father was the cousin of her father, though he'd died when Clarence was small, leaving his mother to raise him. Abby had met the woman on several occasions. She thought her son was the most amazing creature to grace the country of England.

"Then who is Mirabelle?"

"Baron Boxby's wife," she stuttered as his hand tightened. Lord Smith stalked closer. "Highgrove's sister."

"Why don't I know of her?"

He was still shaking her, not paying attention to Lord Smith at all. But the other man was all that Abby could see. He was so tall and strong, his eyes holding hers captive despite the way Clarence shook her...

Meanwhile, Clarence was stealing her air with his anger, making it hard to think. Darkness threatened to engulf her, only the sight of Smith keeping her tethered, his size only seeming to grow larger in comparison as he moved closer.

"She's been gone this past month," she cried, futilely trying to pull back. "I've lived my entire life here in London, Clarence. I couldn't possibly inform you of every contact."

A mistake. She blamed the strength that Lord Smith infused into the air standing so near. As though she might take some of his size and presence as her own.

But she ought to know better. Arguing with Clarence was always a terrible mistake. One she paid for a moment later when his hand came across her cheek, pain exploding through her face, stars sparking behind her eyes.

Her hands flew to cover the spot, cutting through the air to hide the evidence. Protect herself. But her fingers never reached her face. The sickening sound of flesh meeting flesh once again filled her ears, though this time, she wasn't the one who received the hit.

Suddenly, her vision still blurred, she felt herself falling. She hit the floor with a hard thump that knocked the air from her lungs.

She tried to inhale another breath, but she couldn't seem to take in enough to fill her lungs, and the stars she'd been seeing faded to black as the world around her disappeared completely.

———

Well. Fuck.

That's what Rush got for having a moment of happiness. He looked at the baron, sprawled out on the floor from the wicked right hook Rush had landed with perfect accuracy.

The problem? Westphal had been gripping Lady Abigail so tightly, he'd dragged her down too and now…

She'd fallen into a dead faint.

What did he do now?

Did he leave her? Westphal had thought nothing of violently hitting Abigail. When the weasel came to, would he retaliate against the petite woman again?

He looked down at the delicate beauty on the floor, her soft, red lips parted, her eyes closed, and her thick blonde hair half falling from its pins.

He'd promised Mirabelle that he'd look in on her friend, but somehow, he doubted this was what Mirabelle had had in mind.

Still…it was done now. What came next? Did she feel the same way about weasels like Westphal that he did? Did she wish for a different life too? Surely, she didn't wish to stay with this abuser?

But perhaps that was his own gut talking. He felt this pull toward her that he couldn't explain.

He cocked his head, assessing her for another moment. This woman had called to him since the first time they'd met, when she'd come to visit his sister. The feeling was no different today.

He bent down and wrenched Westphal's hand from her upper arm and then placed both his hands over her ridiculously small waist.

Decision made.

Pulling, he easily lifted her limp body, and then he slung her over his shoulder. Her hands slapped limply at the back of his thighs as her face settled against his back, her body folding over him.

The silk of her gown made it more difficult to hold her as she began to slide off his shoulder. He settled her more firmly in his grip, his hand resting on her very round derriere as he started back down the stairs.

The butler stared at him, open-mouthed, as he crossed the entry.

"My lord," he gasped, taking a half step forward. "You can't just—"

"You're going to stop me?" Rush asked, continuing past the man without even pausing, and then he swept out the front door.

The street was quiet as he made his way down the cobblestone walkway from the front door to the sidewalk, where his carriage waited.

Behind him he heard the yelling of the butler, the scurry of footmen. But he ignored both as he wrenched open the carriage door. Ducking into the vehicle, he lowered Abigail to his front before sweeping her legs up to cradle her body against his, then he sat down in his seat, folding her into his lap.

"Go," he ordered the driver.

His words were sharp and commanding. The crack of his voice brooked little argument as the carriage jolted forward.

He didn't have an ornate carriage like many lords. No fancy paint or polished woodwork. His carriage was simple and black, and as they moved onto the busy avenue, he knew he'd blend into the line of other vehicles that clogged the London streets. Which caused him to let out the deep breath he'd been holding, as relief made his shoulders slump.

And then the woman in his arms, in his lap, stirred.

Wide blue eyes blinked open, looking up at him, confusion clouding them as her lips parted. So lovely...and in this moment...his.

"Are you all right?" he asked, admiring the small, straight nose and dark fringe of lashes that framed those blue eyes. Her delicate skin was a perfect shade except for the angry red mark that still graced her cheek.

"All right?" she asked, blinking again as her lips pursed. "I'm not certain. What..." Then she started to sit up.

But he tightened his grip. "Settle, sweetheart," he murmured. It wouldn't do for her to sit up and then faint again. "You've had a shock, I think."

She would be such a lovely partner...if not in crime, then perhaps at the very least in separation, his own true goal. He'd emancipate them both from the tyranny of the peerage and the weight of family that didn't understand them. Surely, she felt that too. After what he'd just seen...she must want to leave as badly as he did.

Rush would take her with him on his new adventure.

"A shock?" she asked, a crease appearing between her brows. Then her hand lifted to her cheek and she winced as her fingers brushed her red skin. "Clarence."

"Is that the little weasel's name?" he asked, a frown pulling at his lips as he looked at her cheek as well. How dare that man mark her. "It suits him."

"I suppose it does," she said, but then the line deepened. "Where is Clarence?" Then she started to sit up. Once again, he held her in place, not wanting her to make the situation worse. "Where am I?"

One of his brows quirked. Wasn't it obvious? "In my carriage."

Her response was to splutter nonsensical syllables as she attempted to once again right herself in his lap. Even big burly men who'd been knocked down had to be careful how soon they got up and so he held her in place. Her gaze snapped up to his as any color that had been returning to her face drained again. See? It was too soon for her to be upright.

"Why..." she asked, the word punching from her lips, "would I"— another gasping breath—"be in"—and finally she grabbed the front of his jacket, wrenching herself up to a sitting position—"your carriage?" He let her go this time.

In his lap, her face came almost even with his and all Rush could think was that she was even prettier this close. Flawless skin, red lips, shimmering eyes.

Her hair was almost out of the pins and the unruly curls tumbled over one shoulder. Almost as if she'd been engaged in a different sort of activity entirely. A very intimate and carnal one.

His manhood twitched and he willed the damn thing to heel. Now was not the time. Except that round derriere that he'd felt with his hand was now pressing into his lap and it was even more delicious like this. He held her tiny waist as he answered, "Because..." He focused on his words instead. "He hit you. Hard."

Her jaw worked as she searched his face. "I understand that, but he is my guardian. It's his right."

"Fuck that," Rush said before he could hold the words back. If his sisters had been here, they surely would have chastised him for swearing in front of a lady. But it was just...these words did not inspire partnership. Didn't she see that Rush had emancipated her? Had he gotten this totally wrong? "I'll not leave you to be hurt like that."

A choked noise erupted from her throat. "But..." And her lips worked, her hands tightening on his coat. "But now..." She gasped, attempting to push out the words.

"What?" he asked, his fingers splaying out on the small of her back. For a woman he'd just rescued, she didn't seem all that grateful. "What's wrong?"

"I'm... I'm ruined. You've ruined me."

He understood the concept of ruining. It was largely an upper-class problem. Most women where he was from gave themselves to a man out of wedlock at some point in their lives. They didn't have the luxury of waiting.

But she was one of them...the elite. A member of the peerage. He'd momentarily forgotten that as he'd held her. Watched her. He'd thought of Abigail like himself, a person looking to escape the situation they'd been trapped in by family…. But clearly, she wasn't.

"You'll be fine."

"I won't," she insisted, her breath hissing out. "He is my guardian. He controls every penny of my dowry, and now…" Her breath trembled. "Turn the carriage around at once. We must go back."

"Go back?" he asked, his voice dripping with disdain. He was angry at her for not being who he'd thought, but even more upset with himself. He should have known she'd never want him. He wasn't part of her world. "How can we go back? Leave you with that abuser? Bow and scrape to that bumptious weasel? I don't think so."

What had Mirabelle done to him? Didn't she know that he should never be left in charge of ladies? He forgot that they didn't fight. They didn't leave… They just accepted whatever shit situation kept them in their comfortable lifestyles with their pretty dresses and their fancy balls.

"We have to go back. If we don't, you'll end up in prison and I'll…" Her breath caught. "I'll be an impoverished spinster. How will I survive?"

"Hell's bells," he gritted out as his hands inadvertently moved down to her hips. He'd forgotten about the feel of her rump in his lap. Holding her was more of a reflex. A vague sense that he needed to protect her despite all the anger that coursed through him.

What was more, she was right about the repercussions in terms of him landing in prison. That was one way to escape his destiny within his family, but not his favorite, to be certain. And what of the position he'd accepted? How would he explain imprisonment to his new employer?

His brother, the marquess, was gone. And his brother-in-law, the baron, had left too, protecting the women of the family.

But clearly, Rush had erred.

He needed help. Whom did he ask?

There was only one man who would know what to do, though asking him would wound Rush's pride more than returning Abigail to that weasel. Still, this moment was no longer just about him. One more obligation he didn't want. One more job he'd never asked for and somehow, it felt as though he were moving further away from the future he was attempting to build for himself.

But he'd have to take the next step anyway. Wasn't that what a man did? He kept going. And so they'd visit his half-brother, the Earl of Easton.

He rapped on the carriage wall. "To East's."

"East?" Abigail asked, giving him the tiniest shake by the lapels of his coat. "What is East?"

"Not what. Who." And then he looked at the woman who'd just upended his life. Had he thought his little interlude with Westphal a break from his problems? From the responsibility that had weighed on him? For that one little moment of freedom, he was about to pay dearly. Of that, he was certain.

CHAPTER THREE

ABBY DREW IN A TREMBLING BREATH, trying to relax despite the tension that pulled her tight enough to snap.

She supposed she might be happy for small favors. Whatever else happened, she'd likely just rid herself of Clarence Westphal forever. But somehow that was little consolation when faced with the possibility of starvation.

She shivered, still seated in Lord's Smith's lap, and he managed to pull her closer still.

The man was an inferno of heat. The tremor that had run through her was from the situation and not from any feeling of chill.

But his body was a distraction. A girl might forget that she was in such trouble this close to all that muscle. "Lord Smith, please—"

"Rush," he corrected, his hand sliding up her back, which caused a whole new set of tremors. "I'm hardly a lord."

Her eyebrows cocked. Truer words… Still, calling him Rush was so…personal. "Rush?"

"Rushton. But none of my family goes by their full given names."

Most lords didn't go by their given names at all. They went by title or family name. The Smiths weren't just casual, they were almost defiantly so, referring to each other by shortened given names. Why was that not surprising?

She tried again. "Rush. Please understand." She forced her fingers holding his lapels to relax, then smoothed the fabric she'd wrinkled up. "I have to go back. Soon. It might already be too late."

"Too late for what?"

"To salvage what's left of my future," she said, though it hardly seemed necessary to speak the words. Were they not obvious?

"That's the future you wish to keep? Living with that rat of a man who thinks hurting women makes him powerful?" He scowled at her as though she clearly hadn't thought the entire thing through.

She had. Every moment since Clarence had entered her life. "Try to understand. I know he isn't a good option, but he's the best one I have. I can't marry another with him as my guardian. He controls every asset in my dowry. I have no means to provide for myself. I am well and truly trapped."

His scowl only grew fiercer. It should have scared her. He looked like a warrior on the brink of battle. But somehow, the look settled her instead. He'd been *her* warrior today. At least for a brief moment.

She slid her hands up the hard edges of his chest, resting them on his shoulders.

"Trapped, are you? I know a bit about that."

This man? Trapped? What might possibly contain him? He'd just stolen a lady in broad daylight.

But she didn't ask as the carriage slowed, turning up the drive of a palatial home that made her own townhouse look tiny in comparison. "Where are we again?"

"I told you. At East's."

East? Her brow furrowed. "I know that you think I should know who that is but…"

He let out a long-suffering breath. "The Earl of Easton."

Her gaze went wide as her stomach turned. "Why are we here?"

"Because." He finally removed one hand from her back to pull the curtain wider. "He is a relation of mine."

Mentally, she tried to marry all she knew about Rush's brother, the

Marquess of Highgrove. He was rumored to be a bastard. "And he can help me?"

"I don't know," Rush answered, his jaw locking tight. "We don't really speak, as a general rule."

Well, that was encouraging. She shook her head as the carriage drew to a stop and then Rush snapped open the door, not waiting for a footman, and lifted her, exiting the carriage. Did he mean to carry her into the earl's entryway?

Strong as he was, it just wasn't done. "Rush," she pushed out, smacking at one of his shoulders. The flesh hardly gave at all, so firm and... "Put me down."

"You're sure you're ready to walk?" he asked, revealing that he truly was worried about her well-being.

It eased some of the worry that had made her chest tight. He truly cared about her physical safety at least. It seemed important, considering she was currently dependent on him for...everything.

"I'm fine," she countered.

But he still didn't set her down. "East has a soft spot for pretty women in need. It's the only reason I even dared to come." He slowed, looking down at her. "You ought to look as injured as possible."

Her lips parted in surprise. Was that why he was carrying her? Her chest constricted again. "We're not lying."

One corner of his mouth tipped down. "It's not lying if I just carry you so that he assumes your injuries are worse."

"But—" she protested, but didn't get out any more words as he started up the stone stairs, jostling her as he trotted up them.

And then he jutted his chin toward the knocker. "You'll have to do it. My hands are full."

"You think?" Still, she reached out and gave the knocker a definite tap. Did she point out that if she were well enough to knock...

He didn't answer and the silence stretched out between them, her lungs growing tighter as they waited. Why was she so nervous? Had she dared to hope this might be an answer...

The door swung open, the butler who answered barely registering, at least outwardly, that a man stood on the stoop with a woman in his

21

arms. Wordlessly, he swung the door wider, stepping back to allow them in.

"I'm—" Rush started but the man held up a hand.

"You're a Smith. I know." And then he turned on his heel and disappeared.

They did not have to wait long before another man appeared at the top of the stairs. And while he was blond-haired and fair in all the ways Rush was dark, the similarities were undeniable: barrel chest, massive shoulders, powerful legs, and a jaw that looked carved from marble.

"Why are you here?" he bit out by way of introduction as he trotted down the stairs.

Abby winced, curling a bit deeper into Rush. Did she speak first? Allow Rush to answer?

"Hello, brother," Rush said as a wave of shock went through her. Brother? Was it just a term of endearment?

But East's face hardened. "Don't call me that."

Rush managed to shrug even as he held her. "Fine."

East's gaze flicked to her and she cringed even further into Rush. "Why have you brought a woman to my house?"

Rush let out a put-upon breath. "I—" he started, the words cutting off as his face twisted into a grimace. "I need help."

East held up his hands. "Ask your actual brother, the marquess."

"He's away with Mirabelle, Anna, and Emily. After the attack…"

Attack? What attack? Her gaze snapped to his.

"Boxby too?" East grunted, his tone a touch softer.

"That's right."

"And who are you holding?" East stopped just a few feet in front of them.

Her tongue darted out to give a nervous swipe over her lips. "I am Miss Abigail Wentworth, my lord. Pleased to make your acquaintance."

But East's eyes grew impossibly wide as his gaze swept back to Rush's. "A lady? Explain this instant."

Oh dear. She wasn't the only one who was angry with Rush. What was going to happen to him now?

————

RUSH FELT his spine stiffen as he held Abigail against his chest. Had he made yet another mistake?

Likely. Not that he regretted his actions. He might not fit into this world, he might hate the elite, but he didn't fear it or its members. In fact, he liked to remind lords regularly that there was power in not caring. "Someone is touchy."

East's nostrils flared and his mouth formed into a thin line. "We've barely spoken before and that is what you have to say to me? Now? As you stand there to beg for my help?"

"I don't beg anyone," he fired back through gritted teeth.

A light tapping started on his shoulder. He looked down to see Abigail staring up at him, her normally wide eyes looking impossibly large and filled with alarm. "Rush," she whispered, though East clearly heard. "Set me down."

With a rumble of frustration, he placed her feet on the marble floor but kept his other arm about her back. She turned to East with a bit of a curtsey. "My sincere apologies, my lord. I am friends with Lady Highgrove and Lady Boxby, and they had asked Lord Smith to check in on me knowing that I find myself in a tenuous situation."

"And what situation is that?" East asked, noticeably softening. See. Rush had been right about his half-brother.

"Her guardian is maggot-filled donkey shit."

He watched as East's gaze traveled over her bruising cheek. "And who did that to you?"

Her lip caught between her teeth as she drew in a breath. "Baron Westphal. My guardian."

East's gaze flicked to Rush but this time, he said nothing except, "Go on."

She folded her hands as she notched her chin higher, in an obvious attempt to be strong. "Lord Smith happened to witness an incident between myself and the baron and he…"

23

"No need to say more. I understand. He took matters into his own hands and swept you away."

She gave a quick nod as East scrubbed his face.

But Rush's jaw snapped up higher. "What was I to do? Leave her alone with that abuser?"

"East?" a woman called from the top of the landing. "Is everything all right?"

"Fine, my love," he called back. Rush looked up to see a stunning blonde at the top of the stairs. Not as beautiful as Abigail, but gorgeous nonetheless.

The woman started down the stairs toward them, her dress flowing out behind her as she did. "What's happened?"

Abigail took a half step back, bumping into him as he tightened his arm about her back. It was better when she was touching him, anyhow. Then he could forget all the ways in which he had made a terrible error. No one liked to thumb his nose at lords more than him and he'd wanted to help her, but he'd let these two factors push him into a series of rash actions that he already regretted.

Still, what else was he supposed to do?

As he listened to East explain to his countess, however, words he didn't like were repeated. Ones like *ruined* and *jail* were bandied about once again.

"I think the question is, what do we do next?" East said looking back at Rush with that same hard expression.

"What did you have in mind?" Rush asked as he ran a hand through his dark hair.

But East only scowled more deeply. "I was hoping you had a suggestion."

Should he? He could hardly seem to manage his own affairs. Wasn't today evidence enough? Then again, he was the one who'd carried her out of her home. Fool. What was it about her that made him forget himself and jump in to aid her? To think that she might be the woman to marry and take away with him? Madness.

"We'll have to speak with her guardian," the countess said with a nod. "See if we can negotiate a settlement where he doesn't press charges and allows Abigail to live somewhere else besides with him."

"Abby," she softly supplied. "My friends call me Abby."

Abby. He liked the name. It suited her. It was pretty and sweet just like the woman pressed to his side. Granted, he'd hoped she'd have a bit more fire. If only she'd wished for rebellion as he did.

"Agreed," East said. "And in the meantime, you'll stay here."

"Good," he grunted, dropping his arm. Abby would be protected here with East and he could return home where he'd regain a clear head. "If you need me—"

East held up his hand. "You're staying too."

He blinked back his surprise. "I beg your pardon?"

"First, you're surely wanted and leaving my house could be dangerous for you."

That was a distinct possibility and one he likely should have thought of. His senses were so damned muddled.

"Second, you are not dropping problems at my door. You brought this situation here, you will help me solve it."

That seemed like a valid point and yet he let out a soft groan. Despite the woman not being what he wished, she was still beyond tempting. "I'll need Gris or Tris to deliver the books. We've still got a club to run." And he had other pressing obligations that needed to be met.

Clearly, he'd not be continuing his investigation into the solicitor who had attacked Mirabelle until he solved the problem of Miss Abigail Wentworth. Now he had two problems to solve before he left London. Granted, this was a nettle of his own making, but he could kick himself. That one moment of wanting her. Of thinking she might be different from the rest, which of course, she wasn't.

East gave a quick nod. "Understood."

Well. At least he agreed on one thing with his estranged brother. That was something. But he'd managed to add another problem to his long list. And in terms of finding his own future…as he looked at Abby, he knew he'd never been less close to finding his place in the world.

CHAPTER FOUR

ABBY CREPT DOWN THE HALL, candle aloft, as she attempted to find her way toward the library. She didn't let out the sigh that held in her lungs, despite the fact that she'd like to. Because the fact that she could not sleep was ridiculous.

For the first time in weeks, a weight had been lifted off her shoulders. In the morning when she woke, there would be no Clarence. No worry of a tirade or of physical violence.

Granted, the fear of the future still loomed large and heavy, but she was getting better at ignoring the persistent worry. For tonight, she wished to enjoy the moment. So she ought to have been able to sleep.

The room that the Earl of Easton had placed her in was large and comfortable, the bed soft, and the crisp night rail that the countess had loaned to her was made of the best cotton. She fingered the fabric with her free hand as a set of double doors came into view up ahead.

All things considered, she should be fast asleep.

But instead, she found herself roaming the halls in a strange house because she was just too…excited. That was the proper word.

Despite her assertion that Lord Smith, or rather Rush, had ruined her, and he had, she was elated to be here. To experience some change. To breathe for the first time in months.

And what was more, she was beyond thrilled with the company of the intriguing man who'd rescued her.

Yes, he was rougher than any lord she knew. Less refined. But something in his behavior was even more titillating. As if he had the raw power to reshape the entire world into the image he wished it to be. To remake her life and transform her situation, make it better.

Could he do that for her? It was a silly hope. Why would he even want to? Except for that he'd saved her. Still, to best Clarence, it would take more than raw male energy. Clarence had the law on his side and he had control of her most cherished asset, Upton Falls. The property was both her dowry and her future. Without it, she'd lose the only place she'd ever been happy.

Stepping into the library, she noted that the fire had been stoked a heartbeat before she saw him. Rush.

He sat in a chair next to the mantel, his legs spread before him, his nightshirt riding up so that his powerful thighs were on full display.

She swallowed a large lump as she attempted to form words.

"Abby," he rumbled from deep in his chest as his gaze rose to meet hers.

Those eyes. They might just captivate a woman's soul if she weren't careful. "Rush." It came out in a squeak as she shifted the candle. "I'm sorry to interrupt. I..."

"Couldn't sleep?"

She shook her head. "You either?"

"I could not." His legs stretched out further from his body, revealing even more of his skin, the muscular length of them, the rough hair that appeared so masculine and... She set down the candle, her hand trembling too much to hold it.

"You're...you're not wearing trousers."

His brows lifted even as he remained relaxed. "If I were home, I wouldn't be wearing anything at all."

The idea of him being naked made a wave of heat roll through her. Futilely, she attempted to change the subject.

"Did...did you need a book too?" She pressed her hands together

27

as she tried not to look at his legs. The large hand that dwarfed the arm of the chair. The hand that had been on her...

"No. I needed whiskey."

She blinked in surprise as he lifted the glass and gave it a little twist, causing the liquid to catch the firelight and wink in the refraction. She wrapped her arms about herself. She wasn't exactly cold. The September nights were chilly, but not with a fire. He was just so...much.

And then he was out of his chair and moving closer. Her breath caught in her throat...trapped. She'd sat in this man's lap today. Rested in his arms.

The memory of him under her, the power in his body, in his actions, had been running through her thoughts all night but especially as she'd attempted to fall asleep. Every time she thought about the feel of him, warm energy flowed through her, making her restless. And here he was...

He stopped a few feet in front of her and then held out the glass. "It will help. Far more than a book."

"I've never..."

He grinned then. It was wicked and wanton and so appealing that a physical ache rolled through her. "Now seems like a good time to start."

That was an excellent point. Tentatively, she took the glass from his hand, their fingers brushing softly as he handed her the crystal snifter.

She tried to ignore the pulsing need the touch caused as she brought the glass to her lips and took a far larger swallow than she ought.

A cough rumbled from her chest and he laughed. "Take another. Trust me."

She did as he commanded and then handed the glass back to him. "It's awful."

That made him chuckle, a low, masculine, and deliciously intimate sound. "It's an acquired taste."

"I'll have to take your word for it," she said with a sigh. "My father never drank whiskey, so I've only ever tried his brandy."

He lifted the glass to his mouth and took another large swallow. "Brandy, heh?"

She shrugged. She'd never thought much of it. But she held up two fingers and then turned them sideways "This amount precisely poured into a snifter every night before bed. I suppose it helped him sleep too."

"Fathers." He shrugged as he turned back to the fire, gesturing for her to follow. "Did you like yours?"

Abby winced as she walked, though Rush couldn't see it. She didn't *not* like her father. "He wished I was a son, I think." The words had popped out, though she hadn't meant them to. She slid into the chair he pointed at, noting that she hadn't been this relaxed in ages.

"A son? Didn't he know that sons are only trouble?"

"I don't know, he never said. And he didn't exactly tell me he wished I were a boy. He just never took any interest in me, so I assumed." Warmth was sliding through her veins and she looked over at Rush, the tug to study him even stronger than it had been before. Was it the whiskey that had loosened her tongue so?

"Interesting. And I do see your point, but that doesn't actually answer my question."

She blinked in surprise. "What?"

"I didn't ask how he felt about you, I asked how you felt about him."

"Oh." She drew in a deep breath, realizing that the warmth had created a happy hum on her thoughts which belied the single word that passed through her lips. "Angry."

———

RUSH QUIRKED a brow as he watched her head tilt back in her chair, exposing the long, delicate column of her neck. He'd like to kiss the length of it. How would she taste? "That's more like it," he murmured, watching the rise and fall of her chest as she took another long swallow.

Watching her drink whiskey was sexy as hell and not at all in keeping with the behavior of a lady. He loved it.

His half-brother had excellent liquor. He had to give the earl that. And East had been angry, but he was helping Rush. That mattered to Rush too. Not that he wished to think of East now. But he had to confess, he usually did for others, not the other way around.

Abby let out a soft sigh that had his muscles tightening with want. "He didn't dislike me," she said, her eyes closed as she continued to stretch out like a cat. "But I'm not sure he ever liked me, either."

His chest tightened with an ache for her, it echoed his own because they had that in common as well. "You were never a priority."

"How did you know?" she asked, her gaze widening as she sat more upright, her large blue eyes fixing on him.

"I know you've heard the rumors," he answered with a shrug. "My father was the Earl of Easton. And I am his bastard son."

She sucked in a breath, her gaze holding his. "That does explain a great deal."

He quirked a small smile. It likely did. "My eldest brother, Ace, was groomed to care for our family. And later, to become a marquess. And Easton was prepared for the earldom. Tris, Gris, and Fulton have all found careers outside of the family, but me…" He didn't belong. He'd not taken to anything. Not the life of a criminal, or a fighter, or a lord. Not a gin distiller or a wine importer, and never a man of the peerage. Not a member of either world.

Before his father had bought them a home in Cheapside, they'd lived near the docks. Cutthroats and ladies of the evening had been their neighbors. And they'd participated in the mayhem. Boys craving trouble, they'd each done deeds that might have landed them in prison or worse.

Hell. They still did. The club, Fulton's occupation… "So your father didn't pay you much mind?"

She shook her head. "Not much. He was too ill at the end for me to have a proper season and now I'm in mourning. As a child, he mostly ignored me. I thought it was just his grief over my mother's death, but then he made no arrangements for me upon his own. I..." Her face tipped forward as she stared at her hands. "No one has ever fought for me before."

Was that what she thought he'd done? Fought? Knocking out Westphal had hardly been a fight. Perhaps she just didn't understand what being a fighter meant... "Are you trying to thank me?"

Even in the dim light, he saw her cheeks heat, turning a soft shade of pink. "I do appreciate it."

"Despite the fact I may have ruined you?"

She shook her head. "There is that. Somehow, being here, I feel less like I'll starve and more like there might be a solution. I'm safe for a moment, anyhow."

He moved his chair closer, reaching out a hand to run it along her forearm. Her skin was achingly soft under his fingertips even as she jumped under his touch.

"You are safe here." How did he explain that she ought to give up on her foolish wish to be a baroness and follow him instead? It wasn't a life like this, but it wasn't starvation, either. They'd have food and shelter and... But even he winced at that idea. He knew he wanted to escape. Wanted to strike out on his own and make his own way in the world, not as his father's bastard son but as a man in his own right. And now he had the new position waiting for him to claim it. Finally. But she would not wish to join him.

He'd been around the peerage long enough to know that independence was far less of a priority than wealth and status.

She looked back up at him, her gaze searching his. "I don't wish to think about tomorrow or the next day. If I do..."

He threaded his fingers through hers. "The world is usually not in one's control."

"Not for you either?"

He thought of all that tied him to London when he so wished to leave. "Most certainly not."

"How can that be?" she asked, giving him a bemused smile. "You seem as though you are Titan."

He chuckled again. "You think I hold up the world?"

"You know your Greek mythology?"

"I'm educated enough, if that's what you're asking." But he withdrew his touch. Was she trying to point out how he was not of her world? Did she believe, as Westphal did, that the peerage was superior? He shouldn't be surprised.

She reached out and grabbed his hand, then locked their fingers together once again. "I wasn't."

He winced, knowing he'd just made an assumption. But all these subtle clues pointed to the fact that it was true. She liked her position, that she shared the views of most members of the *ton*... "Why were you surprised, then?"

"Because you seem like a man more prone to hours spent on horseback than locked in the library with a book."

That was completely fair and absolutely true. Tightening his grip, he tugged her up from the chair and pulled her toward him.

She came easily, a haze in her eyes so that he knew the whiskey had taken effect.

He'd not take advantage. Not really. Just a little.

Settling her in his lap, he groaned deep in his throat as her ass settled in the cradle of his thighs. With only her night rail and his own dressing gown between them, he could feel every curve of her body. She felt even better without the layers and layers of fabric between them. "Believe it or not, of all my brothers, I excel the most at academics. It's how I ended up keeping the books for the club."

She settled her hands on his biceps. "And yet, you act on instinct in a crisis."

"Do I?" he said, but he liked her words, liked even more that he'd saved her today. It made her feel like...well...his. Like she was *his* to protect.

He wished to keep her there, he realized it the moment she settled in. If only she would be happy with the life he could give her, but he already knew that she would not be so. Further evidence as to why he shouldn't have her in his lap like this. She'd get ideas...

He shook his head. The whiskey was going to his head too.

Still, Abby felt better than any woman who'd ever graced his lap—and she saw him too. Understood about his father and the reasons he needed to strike out on his own.

The fire danced off the thick braid of hair that fell over one shoulder, her lips were full and tempting, her scent of lilac and orange filled his nostrils.

He slid his hand up her back, easing her torso closer to his.

"I shouldn't—" she started, her hands tensing on his arms.

"I'd not hurt you, Abby," he murmured in response. She didn't push away but she didn't come closer, either.

"I know you wouldn't mean to," she said in response and then he eased forward, his lips coming in contact with the silky skin at the base of her neck.

He heard her gasp as her chin tipped back a bit to give him more access. That made him smile against her skin as he skimmed his hand higher, winding his fingers around her neck and up into her hair.

Then he tipped her face forward as he kissed a trail up her neck.

"Rush?" she asked. What did she want to know?

"One kiss," he whispered into her skin. "A thank you."

"Thank you?" she asked, but her chin dropped a bit more and then his mouth was brushing against hers.

The kiss was soft and light, her lips achingly smooth as their breath mingled. Despite the lightness of the touch, a jolt of desire coursed through him so strong he nearly crushed her to his chest. It was everything he'd dreamed it would be, which only served to remind him that she wasn't actually his to have.

So he stood, lifting her with him, slowly setting her to the side. "Have another swallow of whiskey and return to your bed."

And then he walked away. Because if he didn't...

Both their futures would be decided. And that set of circumstances wasn't what she wanted.

CHAPTER FIVE

SEPTEMBER SUN, bright and warm, streamed through Abby's window, waking her from a deep and fitful slumber.

Whiskey really did help one sleep.

She pushed back the covers and bounced from the bed. What would today bring? Would the Earl of Easton be able to help her? Would Rush?

What could they do? She fluttered over to the bell cord, ringing for a maid as she began to prepare herself for the day.

What time was it? Was everyone still here? What was the plan for dealing with Clarence? Was the earl's clout enough to cow him?

Hope filled her chest as a maid arrived and helped her dress. She didn't have another dress to wear but the maid carefully pinned up her hair into a loose coif, soft pieces falling about her face, before Abby started downstairs, intent upon finding the breakfast room.

She reached the second-floor landing, pausing to try to remember her way, when she looked over the rail and saw a man standing below.

Broad shoulders. Dark hair. Rippling with muscle. "Rush?"

The man turned, but it was not Rush at all. The eyes were different. The nose. A grin played at his lips though he did not look amused. He looked...dangerous.

Whatever Rush hid under the surface, this man wore outwardly, danger radiating from him like waves in the ocean. "And who are you, little bird?"

She stopped, assessing the man, who was blessedly a floor below. "You must be one of his brothers."

He gave a bow, deep and still mocking, his gaze never leaving hers. "And you must be the reason he's finally made contact with our legitimate brother."

She clapped her hand to her mouth. "I…" she started. She knew it was true.

"Are you also the reason that a constable is stationed outside our home?"

"Oh," she gasped. "Oh dear."

"Indeed," he answered, his arms crossing over his massive chest. He was more of everything from Rush. Larger, more imposing. Scary.

"What should we do?"

"We?" The man's smile grew more wicked.

But a hand touched her back. She half spun, knocking into a large chest. Rush.

The tension winding in her eased.

"My brother will start by minding his own business," Rush said, not sounding worried but bored. Then he looked down into her eyes. "Abby, that is my brother Tris. Lord Triston, to be formal about it."

"The boxer?" she asked, looking back down at the massive man. No wonder.

"She knows about me, does she?" Tris's eyes narrowed. "Why don't I know about her?"

"Likely because you're shit at listening," Rush answered.

Her lips pressed together as an amusement she likely shouldn't feel bubbled up inside her. She was worried for Rush, but the two men together spoke in a way that she'd never heard before and it was fun.

"I'm Miss Abigail Wentworth and I am most pleased to make your acquaintance." She gave the other man a large smile.

"She doesn't even sound like she's pretending," Tris answered, giving her a long stare as Rush let out a growling sigh.

"Did you bring the books?"

"I did. I would have been here earlier, but I had to shake the constable who followed me. I'm going to ask, though I already know the answer. What have you done that you are here and the rest of us are now under surveillance? You know we can't have it."

"It's temporary," Rush said, his hand tightening about her waist. "And just to be clear, the rest of you aren't the only ones who get to make messes that need cleaning in this family."

"I don't know what you mean." Triston's eyes narrowed. "And I didn't ask the length of time, I asked the cause."

"He kidnapped Abby," East called from down the hall as he strode toward them.

Tris quirked a brow. "She looks rather calm and comfortable for a kidnap victim."

East chuckled and she found herself smiling along too.

"It was not a kidnapping. It was a rescue," Rush said as his hand tightened about her. "And it was at our sister's instigation."

Tris lifted up a pile of ledgers he'd set on a table in the entry. "Constables would not be searching for you if it were a rescue."

Tris didn't sound particularly concerned, just irritated, but she found herself uncertain as her gaze shifted to Rush's.

Was he in real trouble? And what did that mean for both of their futures?

He looked down at her, his expression unreadable, as Tris trotted up the stairs. When he approached, he looked even larger, his features hard and unforgiving.

She pressed a bit deeper into Rush, her gaze returning to the man who had protected her. "I can assure you, erm, Lord Triston, that I was not kidnapped."

"Who did that to your face?" he paused, his eyes flicking from Abby to his brother and then back again.

"Her guardian."

Tris frowned. "Does he kick puppies too? What is wrong with some men?"

Much of the air she'd been holding in rushed out of her lungs. "I could absolutely imagine Clarence kicking a puppy if it did not obey his every whim."

"Whether or not he is a good man isn't currently important," East inserted. "What is critical is how we are going to keep Rush from prison and Abigail from Westphal's hands."

"Any ideas? The ones I am entertaining are less than suitable," Rush said, his fingers fanning over her hip.

The touch was exciting but it comforted too. After the way they'd kissed last night and he'd just left, she'd been wondering how things might be between them today.

"I've a few," East said. "Why doesn't Tris join us in my study so that we might discuss them."

Rush gave a quick jerk of his chin to agree and his fingers slipped away. The men turned and left and she watched their retreating backs. What were they about to say? She wished she could attend their conversation. Listen in like a fly upon the wall. Or at the very least, she wished Rush had given her some indication of where they were headed from here.

She might be safe in this moment, but in life, she was completely lost.

————

RUSH's fingers itched to continue to hold her, which he knew was a problem. He'd forced himself to pull away last night but damn, the woman was like the tide...

She was dragging him out to open water whether he wished it or not. And he didn't.

He needed a solid plan moving forward. Instead, he looked back. There she stood, arms wrapped about her torso, looking every inch as though she were lost as well.

He'd attempted to save her already, but she hadn't wished for his help. Outright told him that he'd made a mistake. Abby was too tied to her life in the peerage. She belonged there, after all. Not like him.

He curled his hands into fists as he fought the urge to return to her side.

"I can't fucking believe you," Tris muttered by his side.

His gaze swung over to his brother. "You can't believe what?"

"Ace is one thing—he's a marquess, but you."

Rush stopped, scowling. That was the entire point. He wasn't a marquess. He wasn't anything. "I don't know what you're talking about."

"You've gone sideways for a woman," Tris said, his face hardening.

"I have not." He had. That much was evident.

"Gentlemen," East called as he continued to walk. "We'll continue this conversation in my office."

He gave Tris a small push before he started following East again. He would not tell Tris that he feared his brother was exactly right. It didn't matter that he had feelings for her, though. He was about to make his escape and the more tangled he became in her affairs, the more he jeopardized his carefully laid plans. And she'd already confirmed that she'd not join him. What was left? Would she change her mind if he asked?

"Gentlemen?" Tris rumbled from behind him. "He doesn't know us at all, if he is calling us that."

Rush looked over his shoulder, a bit of dissatisfaction trickling down his spine. "I'm a glorified accountant. That makes me a gentleman, does it not?" That was the problem. He craved more. He thought again of the position he'd accepted. It seemed further away than ever.

Tris's nose wrinkled in disgust. "You are not. You're..." But his brother tapered off making Rush's point.

East pushed open a door on the left, revealing a rich and masculine study beyond. The room's dark wood paneling and leather furnishings spoke of comfort and of wealth. Rush stopped, realizing that he liked the room immensely. It would be comfortable to spend afternoons in a room such as this, working on the books. He forced his thoughts in a different direction. He'd saved a fair bit from the work at the club, and he'd continue to save while working in his new position in the country, but it would be many years before he came the master of his own home and lands. And even then, his life would never mirror this.

Besides, he hated accounting. It was a necessary part of his life now and in the future, but no room would make the task enjoyable.

But as he slid into one of the overstuffed chairs, he amended his thought. He didn't mind accounting. Truly. He just needed the activity to be paired with something more physical and something more…meaningful.

Perhaps just in pursuit of his own success instead of the success of his family.

"My first question is…" East said from the chair across from Rush. "What are your intentions toward Abigail?"

"My intentions?" he asked with a scoff. "You ought to ask her that question."

Tris made a rumbling objection but Rush lifted his hand to stop his brother. "She told me yesterday that I ruined her life despite the fact that I stopped a vicious attack on her person."

East cocked his head. "Ruined her life or ruined her reputation?"

"What's the difference?" Tris asked, articulating the very question that had been rattling around Rush's thoughts.

"A woman needs her reputation to marry…well, anyone."

"Anyone of the peerage," Rush amended. "Which to her might mean anyone of worth, but it is a separate issue."

"Not really," East said, giving him a hard scowl as he shifted in his seat. "Because her guardian controls her dowry and has to give permission for her to wed, it's his opinion that matters, not hers. She might be content to marry the baker, but if Westphal refuses the match, she has no choice but to remain unwed or marry him regardless and forfeit her dowry. And then, should the baker die first, she has only the money he's left her to survive. Many a woman has been left in dire straits as a widow. And that does not just include the upper class."

Rush winced, wondering for the first time if he'd misunderstood Abby's reaction. He'd been hurt in that instant. He knew that and perhaps he'd been quick to judge. He was so used to not quite belonging that he'd just assumed.

He didn't belong with her, either.

He wasn't special to his father. Wasn't notable in his family, and he'd not be the man whom Abby chose. He was destined to be the other...

Wasn't he? She had kissed him last night. Slipped into his lap and drank whiskey, of all things, with him. Did that mean something? "So what are you suggesting?"

"I'm not suggesting anything. Her options are very limited."

"So if she marries anyone but Westphal, she has to give up all her money?" Tris asked, making a face. "That's a pile of shit."

"Agreed," East said with a nod. "But that's the way it's done. She can marry a man who would provide for her regardless, if she could find one who'd agree..." And then East gave him a long, meaningful look, his head cocking to the side.

Rush's brows shot up. "And how would I replace a dowry like that?"

But East didn't answer. "You could make an offer. Westphal will refuse. He might even call you out in a duel."

"Let him," Rush said, his hand slashing through the air. "The man deserves a bullet after the way he treated her."

"You heard the part where he said you needed to offer first, didn't you?" Tris rumbled.

Would she accept if she thought that he could access her dowry? It was an interesting idea that she didn't care about his lineage, just her fortune. As a man who'd struggled with the family's finances for years, that was a problem he could understand. He'd truly suffered poverty and lived amongst the worst of society and he'd not wish that on anyone.

Perhaps it was time to speak with Abby again.

"So the solution is for my brother to challenge Westphal?" Tris asked.

"He did kidnap a woman from Westphal's home."

"I already told you. It wasn't kidnapping. It was a rescue," he gritted out.

"But we might be able to avoid such a confrontation if we bring some real social sway with us to speak with him."

"Social sway?" He didn't need other men to fight his battles for him.

But Tris was shaking his head. "I say we just kill him outright. How bad could it be?"

Then again, perhaps another man besides Tris, someone with a bit less bloodlust, might help. "You can't just go around killing barons," he admonished Tris before he looked at East. "Who did you have in mind to ask for help?"

"Normally, I'd bring one of my friends, but most of them are still in the country."

Lucky them. He'd like to be in the country now. Riding, smelling the clean air. Away from gaming hells and barons who hurt women.

"So perhaps one of our fellow owners. What about the Duke of Upton?"

Upton? He'd do.

"And what are we going to say?" Tris asked. "I still think we ought to just shoot him."

Rush rolled his eyes. "This isn't the East India docks."

Tris shrugged. "He still deserves it."

Rush shook his head. Tris wasn't wrong. But despite his dislike of all things connected to the peerage, he wasn't fool enough to do something as rash as just kill Westphal.

Abby needed Rush to use his head, and if he'd been one thing, it was her warrior. And he'd do so again. Which meant thinking his way out of this mess.

CHAPTER SIX

ABBY WAS STILL STANDING in the spot the men had left her when a soft voice called from behind. "Are you all right?"

"I'm not certain," she answered honestly before she pulled herself together. She turned to see the countess standing behind her. Pulling her shoulders straighter, she plastered a smile on her face. "Thank you for your generous hospitality, my lady."

"Please. Call me Lily." The other woman gave her a beautiful smile. "And you're very welcome."

"Abby," she said as she reached out a hand.

"Abby. I'm glad you're here," Lily said, taking Abby's hand in both of hers.

Abby's lips parted in surprise. Could that really be true? "That is so kind of you to say. But sincerely, you needn't."

The other woman took her fingers, gently grasping Abby's. "I know a bit about being in a dire situation."

Abby blinked in surprise. The beautiful countess before her had the entire world at her feet. "You do?"

"I do," she said and leaned in, her voice dropping to a whisper. "I did not grow up in the peerage and there were times that I could hardly provide for myself."

Abby gasped in surprise, allowing Lily to lead her to a nearby sitting room. "What did you do?"

"I took my life one day at a time and then..." They entered the room, sitting on a settee across from the fire. She leaned forward, her eyes sparkling. "My husband happened upon me in a dire time and he rescued me."

A thrill pulsed through Abby. "Like what Rush did for me?"

"Precisely." Lily nodded. "I don't know what more you could ask for in a man than that."

But that only made Abby wince. "I agree."

"Do you?"

Abby nodded. "The problem is that I have so little to give. My guardian holds my dowry and without his consent, I'd bring nothing to the match." And she'd lose the one place in the world she actually loved—Upton Falls. Had her father known that she felt that way when he'd made the property her dowry? It was something to consider, just not at this precise moment.

But Lily only cocked a brow. "Is that what concerns you?"

Abby nodded. It was one of many ideas that troubled her. "I have so little to give, not that he even wants me, because I don't think he does."

"Nonsense." Lily waved her hand. "Men don't go about rescuing women they don't want, even if they don't admit their feelings for a while."

"Why do you say that?" she asked, cocking her head to the side.

"Because." Lily looked up as she paused to think. "Rescuing a woman is a great risk. They don't put themselves in that sort of danger lightly. If he did, it's because you're important. Even if he's been too stubborn to admit that fact yet."

"I don't think so," Abby shook her head. "He said that Mirabelle sent him to check on me. That's why he came. What's more, he made a snap decision. It's not like he set out to rescue me."

"Does he normally take such risks?"

That was a good question. One to which she didn't know the

answer. But even as she considered how to ask, male voices filtered down the hall and soon, the men appeared by the door.

Abby rose, catching sight of Rush. Was what Lily had said true? Did he value her in some way? Want her?

His gaze caught hers and he entered the room, reaching out a hand to her. "Are you all right?"

There it was. His concern. Surely he cared some if he was so worried. Her breath caught. She cared too. This man had put himself between her and the greatest danger she'd ever faced and he'd done so without asking a thing from her.

And they had some sort of kinship that they shared. Perhaps it was their issues with their fathers, but there was something that drew them together. She could feel their connection. "I'm fine."

He gave a quick nod. "We'll get this sorted soon enough."

Would they? Had they come up with some sort of plan? Was he going to once again act on her behalf? "What are you going to do?"

He looked down at her. "Nothing you need worry about."

"Tell me." She'd feel better knowing.

He lightly touched her cheek before he dropped his hand again. "We're going to go speak with Westphal."

Her stomach gave a nervous flutter. "He's got an awful temper. I'm not sure you should go."

A small, charming smile tugged at his lips. "Are you worried about me?"

"Yes," she answered honestly. "I can't have you getting hurt on my account."

He shook his head. "I'll be fine. Westphal doesn't frighten me."

"He frightens me," she whispered. "And I'd never forgive myself if something happened to you…"

His smile grew wider as he moved closer. "I will be absolutely fine. It's you I've got to worry about."

Something warm slid through her at those words. "I appreciate your concern, but I'm still worried."

He shook his head and then leaned closer. "We're going to bring the Duke of Upton and I'll have Easton as well. Westphal will surely respect the titles, even if he doesn't me."

That did make her feel a bit better, though Lily's words were settling more deeply in her thoughts. Did Rush care? He was going through a great deal of trouble. And he'd kissed her last night. She'd like to ask. "There is so much I wish to say…"

He gave a quick nod and then leaned close and whispered in her ear. "Meet me tonight. You know where."

Her breath caught as her heartbeat thrummed in her ears. That was an excellent idea. They could talk. He could tell her about the meeting with Clarence and she could ask about his feelings. Share hers.

But as appealing as all that sounded, what she thought of most was that kiss. And how much she'd like another.

———

THE CARRIAGE RIDE to Upton's was completed in near silence. Though East was their half-brother, now that they'd decided how to proceed with Abby's protection, the three men didn't know what to say to one another.

Tris shifted, his legs spread wide in front of him as he leaned back in his seat. "There was an incident at the club last night."

"What kind of incident?" Rush sat up straighter. He might want to leave the club and his family behind, but that club had given him the means to do so and his family depended on that income. It was slowly lifting them up…

Which is why he'd see that lawyer found and stopped before he left them. Just like he'd see Abby settled. Hopefully, his future would still be there when he was finished.

Tris cleared his throat. "Gris was the one who was working, so my account isn't firsthand."

"Tell me," Rush asked. East shifted in the seat across from them.

"A man came in claiming to be the buyer of the club. Demanded access to the back room. Gris tossed him out but in his Gris way."

"Why didn't he hold the man? Come get me for questioning?"

"The club was extraordinarily busy, Gris was alone, and you were not at home."

His jaw clenched. He'd taken his eye off the club for a few days. How had his brothers managed to ruin his chance to find the perpetrator that kept him tied to his family? "Busy?"

Tris grimaced. "We'll catch him. Don't worry."

"Our brother has left London with our sisters. Doesn't this seem like a pressing problem to you?" His hands clenched into fists. "Why didn't you tell me sooner?"

"We've been a little busy talking about you," Tris fired back, fire lighting in his eyes. "This investigation is supposed to be your job."

"Why is my job always the family?"

"You don't have anything else."

He hit his thigh, his fist still clenched tight. "So if I did have something else, you'd pay more attention to the business and less time having your face smashed in?"

"What does that mean?"

"We both know that the club keeps you in your pretty clothes, not your time in the ring. Be honest, Tris. You don't care about me being single, except that it would distract me from providing for you."

Tris's face turned a dark shade of red that Rush knew meant he'd dug into a wound. And that his brother was likely to punch him. Which was fine. He'd been itching for a fight. And maybe the pain would distract him from the desire coursing through him thanks to Abby.

But East's voice cut through their argument. "Not in my carriage."

Tris slowly returned to a more normal color, his features slowly softening. When he'd relaxed again, he reached into his jacket. "Gris did manage to collect a slip of paper from the man's pocket."

He pulled out the folded-up sheet and handed it to Rush.

Rush looked at the sheet. Would it provide any answers? But he didn't have a chance to discover more as the carriage arrived at Upton's.

East exited first. "It's early enough that the duke should be home."

Rush hoped so. He needed to check one problem off the list swirling about him.

CHAPTER SEVEN

AN HOUR LATER, they stood outside the home of Westphal, Rush's chest heavy with the anger that beat against his ribs.

He was upset with his family, furious beyond measure at the audacity of Westphal for raising a hand to Abby to begin with, and wondering if he was ever going to untangle himself from the mess in which he'd landed.

He'd wanted out of this life with his family, but mostly, as he looked up at the house before him, he had a flash of how he might have to remain in it forever. If he did, he could provide for Abby without a dowry and without her guardian's permission. Then he'd remain his brothers' provider forever as well. But then, he'd lose his new position, and everyone but him would get what he or she needed.

Forever the brother least noticed, least accomplished. Had his father known that was what he was creating in Rush?

He drew in a rumbling breath as he started up the stairs.

"Remember," Upton rasped, having been caught up on all the events that had transpired in the carriage ride to Westphal's, "keep your cool."

"Cool?" Tris groused. "I say give him hell."

"You are not helping," East said to Tris. "Stop or I'm sending you home."

"You don't get to send me anywhere," Tris growled. "You're not Ace or even Rush."

"Even Rush," Rush snorted, as if Tris's comment underscored his inner thoughts. "East gets to send you home whenever it pleases him." And then he hastened up the stairs, pounding with the knocker.

The butler opened the door, taking a half step back at the sight of Rush, who took full advantage, stepping inside before the man could recover. "Lord Smith, Lord Triston, the Duke of Upton, and the Earl of Easton here to see Baron Westphal."

The butler muttered out some incoherent response before he rushed off.

Westphal appeared moments later, once again standing at the top of the stairs. "Where is my ward?"

"Safe."

Westphal's face went purple. "Return her this instant."

"No." Rush's chest expanded. "Not happening."

"You'll be arrested and—"

"And what?" He gritted out the words around clenched teeth. "Do you see the men behind me? Have me arrested and they, along with my many other associates among the peerage, will make certain you never belong. Not ever."

He watched Westphal's face go ashen and he knew he'd hit the mark. If Westphal cared about one thing, it was his own worth. "You can't have her. She's mine."

His teeth gnashed back and forth. He'd give everything up before he'd allow that to happen. Everything. It beat through his veins right along with his blood. He'd chain himself to that desk and to his family before he'd allow this man to have Abby back. "Not yours. Never again."

East came to stand next to him, tall and straight as he gave Rush the smallest nod.

"I am her guardian. You don't get to decide."

"I told you." He narrowed his gaze, glaring, every muscle rigid. "You don't have a choice if you want to keep your standing in the *ton*."

The other man banged his hand several times on the banister as he made his way down the stairs. "I'll see you hang," Westphal yelled, spit flying from his mouth as he reached the bottom of the stairs.

"I'll see you ostracized," he replied as calmly as he could. The anger bubbled inside but he pushed it down. He'd control himself now.

Westphal stopped, teeth grinding. "No. You will not."

"Then find another woman to marry."

"But her land—" The other man stopped and Rush paused. Land? What was that about land? But then Westphal seemed to recover. "You leave me no choice but to challenge you."

"Fine by me." He could use a fight. Every muscle tensed in readiness. "Choose your weapon."

"Rush," East said softly but it was too late. His blood boiled, and besides, he'd made up his mind. He'd defend Abby with all that he possessed. That included but was not limited to his own person.

"Pistol," Westphal answered. "Winner gets the hand of Abigail."

He gave a stiff nod, glad they'd reached this point so quickly. "First light in Hyde Park."

"I shall see you then. You may see yourself out."

Rush only watched Westphal's retreating back for a moment before he turned, leading the way out the door, Tris falling in step next to him. "You're fighting for her hand?"

"Trust me," Rush answered. "You're hoping I'll win?"

"Of course I am," Tris spit on the steps. "I would prefer you not be dead."

"I'm not going to die, but if I win, and Abby stays with me, then I stay here. I stay with you. If she goes, then so do I."

"Go where?" his brother asked, his hand shooting out to stop Rush. "Where would you go? What the fuck are you talking about?"

Was this the time to tell his brother his plans? "I've found another job. Another life. Like you, and Gris, and Fulton." Had he never told his brother these thoughts? But Tris fell silent as Rush stopped in front of the carriage, allowing Upton and East to enter first.

"Another life? Away from us or here in London?"

His jaw locked tighter. "Why don't we discuss this after the duel?"

"I want to know now." Tris grabbed his arm, his face right in Rush's face. "Tell me what you've planned."

"As I said. It all might be a moot point. If I win…"

"I'll be your second," Tris said, easing back, though the strain about his eyes remained. "Gris is better with a pistol, but I'll keep you safe before the duel."

Rush gave a tight nod. "Thanks."

"Rush," Tris started, "why would you leave now? We've just started to gain traction financially. We'll be able to move soon and—"

He cut his brother off with a look. "You've always been able to find your own way. A career in boxing. Minimal involvement in the club. Has it ever occurred to you that I might wish the same?"

Tris seemed to contemplate Rush's words. "And you'd give up this future for her?"

"I can't let him have her…" He'd not tell his brother that he'd hoped she'd be braver. Instead, he settled into the seat. "She'd make staying worthwhile." She'd make staying more enjoyable at the very least. Marriage would give him purpose, though not the one of which he'd dreamed.

Tris didn't answer as the carriage started back down the road toward East's home. He'd begun today certain he wouldn't marry, and now he was convinced that he would. How strange. But somehow, facing Westphal again, he just knew. Perhaps his lot in life was to provide for others. And Abby would be worth whatever he sacrificed. At least if he were chained to a desk, he'd end the day with her snug in his lap.

―――――

WAITING until the house had quieted was a small form of torture, Abby decided as the clock stuck one in the morning.

Finally, she opened her door with a slowness that made her breath hold in her chest.

Creeping down the hall, she made her way to the library.

Rush and East had returned in the early evening, but then the two men had sequestered themselves in East's office.

She walked along the dark halls and entered the library, relief making her shoulders limp when she found Rush sitting in the same chair, once again sipping whiskey. "Rush."

He stood, setting down his glass and opening his arms to her. Without hesitation, she ran into them, burrowing into his chest. "You're all right." She'd been filled with nagging fear all day. And while it had abated when he'd arrived back at Easton's home, seeing him made something tight that had been coiled inside her unwind.

"I'm fine," he murmured against her hair. "And so are you."

She nodded into his chest. "Thank goodness."

"I don't want you to worry," he said, his lips grazing her forehead. "I'm going to take care of it."

"Take care of it?" she asked, tipping her chin up to look at him. But rather than answer, he bent down, his lips brushing hers.

How were this man's lips so wonderfully comforting and exciting all in the same light touch? She slipped her arms about his neck as he kissed her again, deeper and longer. It was less of a brush and more of a press, making the excitement in her belly expand and sink, settling as an ache between her legs.

He held Abby tighter to him as he kissed her a third time, parting her lips and running his tongue along their seam.

She gasped, opening wider as his tongue made another pass. Abby pressed into him, the sensation ricocheting through her enough to melt her bones.

His hands fisted into her night rail at the small of her back as he held her close. His muscles seemed to surround her as her fingers danced up his neck and into his hair.

When his tongue made another pass, she was ready and she opened fully to him, her own tongue meeting the thrust of his.

His answering groan told her that he enjoyed the touch as much as she did. Her fingers tightened, grasping the short strands of his hair in back as the kiss went on and on, their tongues tangled, and he pulled her closer still.

No one had ever made her feel like this. How did he do it?

But that only led her muddled mind to other questions. Ones like *How would he keep her from Clarence?*

"Rush?" she said between kisses. "Tell me what happened today."

He sighed into her mouth, but his kisses slowed. "I'll have to win your hand."

Shock coursed through her. Her hand? "What does that mean?"

His eyes closed, his forehead resting on hers. "Your choices are me or him."

"But…" She swallowed down a lump. "How is that even possible? He's my guardian."

"He knows I'm well-connected and I threatened to have him ostracized from society. So he's agreed to a duel, winner take all."

"A duel!" She wrenched back from his grip. "You can't fight in a duel."

"I can and I will," he answered, his gaze unwavering. "The only other choice is to give you back, and no matter what each of us wanted for our futures, I won't do that."

What each of them wanted? Those words sat like a lead ball in her stomach. "What did you want, Rush? What was it you wished for that you'd be giving up?"

He shrugged. "It doesn't matter now."

"Does it have to do with your father?" She barely pushed the words past her lips as she stepped toward him again and held on to him like a woman drowning.

"It started there, yes. I wanted him to love me as much as he did Ace, so I always…" He stopped, looking into the fire. "At some point I realized I'd spent my entire life giving to my family and I'd not done a thing for myself."

"And what would you do for yourself?"

He shook his head. "I've found a job managing a property—" But he stopped, his jaw hardening. "It doesn't matter. Tomorrow, I will win. And then we'll marry. I won't need your dowry. The club will provide all that we need and more."

But it did matter. It mattered very much to her. "You can't marry me if it isn't what you wish."

"You'd marry him, wouldn't you? I know you don't want to, but you would."

"Yes, but I don't have a choice. The alternative is to—"

"Be cast from society?"

What did that even mean? And why would that matter? "No."

But he kissed her again. Short and hard, his hands cupping her cheeks. "I'm sorry that I cast the die before you had a choice. But I can assure you that life with me will be better than it ever was with him."

"I have no doubt—"

"You don't?"

"Of course not. But—"

His next kiss wiped her mind of thought. The touch was long and desperate, and she melted again. When he finally lifted his face, he stared down at her, his gaze dark and glittering. "I need to leave in a few short hours, sweetheart, so I should go to bed. But know that I'll do the best I can for you, Abby."

He started to walk away but it felt too much like the last night. "Not yet."

He stopped, turning back to her, and she tried to articulate all the reasons this felt wrong.

"What is it?"

She shook her head. "I'd be lucky to have a husband like you, Rush. Any woman would."

He relaxed a bit, his shoulders slumping as a small smile touched his lips. "Good."

"You fight for the people you care about."

"I try," he said, stepping close again, his hand trailing over her cheek. "But I appreciate that you see that. And I promise. I'll fight for you too."

But she had to wonder. Who was fighting for him?

She drew in a deep breath before she reached up on tiptoe and kissed him again. "I want to come."

"Where?"

"To the duel. I want to come."

"No," he said with a shake of his head. "It's no place for a woman."

She heard the words, she truly did. But she was tired of being a victim and even more tired of watching men decide her fate. Tomorrow, she'd fight too.

There was no winning for her. She knew that. But Rush still could. And he would. She'd see to that at the very least.

CHAPTER EIGHT

ABBY TUGGED at the breeches currently hugging her legs and frowned. Did men find these comfortable?

The sun had not yet risen and she'd yet to fall asleep, but there was no time for that now. She had to go to that duel. And after an hour of thinking—and a few sips of whiskey—this was all she'd managed to come up with.

She'd gone to the storage room by the kitchen and found spare clothes for a footman. She studied herself in the candlelight, noting that the breeches did mold themselves to her behind in a flattering way, but she'd never felt more exposed.

Would anyone mistake her for a boy? She'd have to stay well out of sight. But she'd not get anywhere in skirts, she knew that much.

Tucking the braid of her hair into her shirt, she pulled on the tail-coat and then the bicorne hat, hoping no one noticed she bore no wig. It would be dark enough, she mused, and her hair was thick enough to be mistaken for a wig without too much light.

With that in mind, she snuck downstairs by way of the servant's stairs, down to the kitchen and out the back door to the stables.

As the carriage made its way out of the stable and along the narrow drive, she followed and watched from the shadows as Rush,

Tris, and East all climbed in. Then, slipping through the darkness, she climbed on the seat in the back of the carriage and let out a long breath.

Thank goodness they'd not brought any other servants with them, or she would have been running.

The carriage rumbled along the silent streets as she held on, wondering where they were headed. But her brow wrinkled with confusion as they stopped in front of a stately manor near Easton's home.

And then the front door opened, and a man came striding toward them.

Drat. Had he seen her? She slipped off the seat and around the back side of the carriage, sighing with relief when he entered the vehicle. Then she climbed back up onto her seat and the carriage started again.

Only, it hadn't gone more than few hundred paces when it drew to a stop again. The door crashed open and Tris appeared before her. He didn't say a word as he hauled her by the shirt collar off the seat and to the ground, where her legs promptly buckled.

She'd known the man was strong, but the raw power of his body had her quaking in her Hessians as her hands came to his, gripping his wrist in an attempt to stay upright.

"Tris," she cried, trying to catch her breath as her feet scraped on the cobblestone.

But she heard Rush let out a string of curses as he exited the carriage too. "Abby?"

"Abby?" Tris repeated, loosening his hold. "Really?" And then he peered down at her face, letting out a booming laugh. "Clever girl." His grip instantly eased as he brought his other hand under her armpit and then pulled her back to standing, straightening her coat.

She might have smiled in appreciation, but Rush appeared next to her, knocking her brother's hand away. "I told you not to come."

"When did you tell her that?" East asked from the interior of the carriage.

But Upton stuck his head out, interrupting all of them. "Let's go.

We need to have this business done while the light is still dim. Both for your advantage during the duel and so that no one goes to prison."

Rush only growled. "We have to take her home first."

Home. Easton's house was not their home. But her chest still swelled at the idea of any home she might have with Rush. It would be so easy...so easy to love him and let him save her. If she were being honest, she loved him already.

That knowledge swelled in her chest as she looked at him. "Please, Rush. I'll stay in the carriage, I swear it. I just need to be there."

She had no intention of staying in the carriage.

In fact, she had no intention of allowing the duel to happen at all. But she didn't say any of that to Rush.

Because she knew exactly what sort of man he was. He'd squash her plans and fall on his sword to protect her. Well, in this case, it was a pistol, but her point stood.

Rush looked undecided for a few moments but finally gave a quick nod. "Tris is my second, so either Upton or East can stay in the carriage with you."

Drat. That wouldn't do. She gave him a quick smile. "Shouldn't they be with you? Keeping you safe?"

Rush raised an eyebrow. "Westphal is not that frightening, sweetheart."

He was to her. But the endearment had her sighing rather than answering. How did one word from his lips make her forget all her plans? Abby needed to think. How was she going to enact her plan with a duke or an earl as a guard? She didn't know Upton at all, but East...

He had a soft spot for women in need.

She settled between Rush and Tris, her breath trembling out of her lungs.

"You're not a fainter, are you?" Tris asked with a grunt. "I'm not much for women who faint and there is likely to be blood. Is blood going to bother you?"

"What?" she asked, swallowing down a lump of fear before she pushed her shoulders back and attempted to harden her resolve. She did not want to see Rush's blood. That was the entire reason she was here.

"She is," Rush answered for her. "A fainter."

"That's not fair," she said. "I'd just been hit and then you punched Westphal and he pulled me down, making me bump my head." Her chin jutted up. The last thing she needed was to be reminded of her weakness now. Her hand automatically came up to the note she'd slipped into her breast pocket. It would explain her reasons to Rush later.

Rush reached for her hand, clasping it in his own. Perhaps it was the tiredness, but the feel of his fingers around hers made her weepy. She held in the tears as she looked over at him. Would this be the last time she'd ever touch him like this?

He pulled her close and she rested her cheek on his shoulder, breathing in his scent. She wanted to remember this moment forever. She wanted to remember him forever—in case something happened. No, she told herself inwardly. She wouldn't let anything happen to him.

The carriage entered Hyde Park and conversation ceased as the wheels rumbled down the carriage path. All too soon the vehicle stopped and Abby held her breath as Rush turned to East. "Stay with her."

"Of course." East remained in his seat as the other three men stepped out.

"How long?" she asked East, shifting on the bench, peering out the curtain into the foggy darkness.

"Not long," he answered, crossing his feet in front of him. "And try not to worry. I don't know Rush well, but I know he is the sort of man who can take care of himself."

She didn't reply. Westphal's voice cut through the darkness. "You came."

Rush answered but the words were drowned out by her own shaky breath as she studied the man in front of her. Tentatively, she pulled out the letter she'd hidden in her coat. "I need to ask you a favor."

His brows lifted as she handed him the paper. "What is this?"

"For Rush," she said, handing him the folded sheet.

But his brow crinkled in confusion. "You're going to see him after. He'll not be hurt, I'm sure of it."

"I know he won't be hurt because I will not allow that to happen," she said and then she pushed the carriage door open and bolted out before the earl could stop her.

———

RUSH WATCHED Westphal walk into view. "He's here," he muttered to Tris. "I half expected him to be too cowardly to even arrive."

"And let you ruin his reputation?" Tris snorted. "I don't think so."

"Fair point."

"In terms of strategy, I say you let him fire first. My gut tells me he'll shoot off prematurely." Rush looked back at his brother as Tris gave him a meaningful stare. "Then you can take whatever shot you wish. Are you going to injure or kill?"

"Injure," he answered with a grimace. "Much as I'd like to never have to look at his face again, I don't want there to be any more scandal than necessary where Abby is concerned."

Tris nodded as he looked back at the carriage. "You like her that much?"

"Enough to not risk scandal?"

"Enough to give up your freedom. All of it."

He did. In fact, he far more than liked her. Upton opened the case with the pistols inside as Westphal approached.

"You're here," the other man said, his second standing at his left shoulder.

"Did you doubt it?"

"I don't know. I thought a man who stole women wouldn't have the honor to fight for her."

Rush bristled. "I wasn't stealing—"

But his words were cut off by a much more feminine voice. "It was a rescue." Abby. What was she doing out of the carriage?

She came striding toward them, looking adorable in the short breeches and coat. How did she manage that?

"Back in the carriage," he barked as Westphal pivoted toward her. East was just behind her, looking both irritated and apologetic.

"Good," Westphal said, eyeing her, "this will make your collection easier."

Good? Did the man not care for her well-being at all?

She stopped a few feet from them, her eyes locked on Rush's, her gaze silently pleading. What was she asking for?

But her voice was resolute as she called out, "There will be no duel today."

Fear bristled down his spine as he took a step toward her. "Abby." What was she doing? "Get back in the carriage. East, take her—"

"No one is dying for me." She shook her head and held up her hands. "Especially not you, Rush. I would never forgive myself."

"I've no intention of dying." He took another step toward her, intent upon putting himself between her and Westphal. East reached her side, his hand coming to her arm.

"I'm going to kill you," Westphal replied, his lip curling. "Make no mistake."

"No, you're not," Abby answered, her voice trembling with obvious fear. "And in exchange, Clarence, I'll come with you."

A growl ripped from Rush's chest, fear pounding through his veins. For the first time since he'd arrived here, he was afraid. "What did you just say?"

"I'm going with Baron Westphal," she said, her voice full of pleading that set his teeth on edge. What did she wish for him to understand—how she could not give up being a baroness?

How had he been such a fool? He'd been willing to give up everything to be with her. Everything that had ever been important. "Abby." It came out as a snarl and she flinched.

"Please understand."

"Oh, I do," he said with a deadly quiet that belied the anger filling him with liquid hot rage. Even after everything he'd willingly give up for her, she was going to choose her standing in society over him. How had he allowed himself to be the least wanted once again?

She shook her head. "Understand that I—"

"Enough," Westphal said, wrapping a hand around her upper arm. Even now, Rush could barely stand the sight of that man touching her.

He ached to rip the other man's hand from her arm and pull her close. His fists clenched as he took a half step forward. "Don't do this."

"Rush." Her voice held a pleading that forced his gaze to hers. "You deserve the best."

What the hell did that mean? Another shit consolation meant to appease him for being her fool?

Westphal spit between them. "He deserves nothing." And then he gave Abby a yank and she stumbled toward his second. "Put her in the carriage," Westphal ordered as he took a step back.

The other man began pulling Abby toward Westphal's carriage and for a moment, he watched her go, torn between the hurt that ripped through him and the need to protect her still.

His anger and hurt distracted him, his eyes were glued to her back so that he didn't notice Westphal reach into his coat. Didn't see the first rays of sun glint off the barrel of the pistol Westphal pulled out.

It wasn't until Tris gave him a hard shove at the same moment that an explosion filled the air that he realized Westphal had fired at him. Attempted to kill him despite the fact that he was unarmed, the dueling pistols still tucked within their case.

He let out a war cry even as he heard Tris's grunt.

A scream rent the air as Abby attempted to pull away and return to him. He hit the ground hard as Westphal sprinted away, helping to push Abby into his own carriage. "Stop him!" Rush yelled and Upton lit out after them, East falling just a step behind.

He hauled himself up from the ground and started after them too as Westphal's carriage sprang into motion.

Abby. It didn't even matter that she didn't want him. She had given herself to a man without principle. Without honor.

"To the carriage," he cried out, looking back at his brother. Tris held his arm as blood gushed from a wound.

"Go without me," Tris gritted out.

Rush stopped for a moment, staring.

"Go," Tris yelled again.

"Get in the fucking carriage," he growled, grabbing his brother's other arm. "I'd sooner take a ball to the chest than leave you here."

But his problems were still multiplying. He wrenched an arm under his brother's armpit and they hefted him toward the carriage, as Tris grunted in pain. "Where do you think he's taking her?"

"I don't know," he answered while Upton stepped up to Tris's other side. "Back to his home? To another property? I have no idea."

"She knew she was going to do it," East offered. "She left you a note."

He grimaced, not even certain he wished to see the words that explained. Would they only dig deeper into the wound she'd just opened?

They reached the carriage, and helping Tris in, he climbed in too. East entered and held out a slip of paper.

He settled into his seat, tucking the sheet in his pocket, not ready to face the words as he attempted to assess his brother's wound. Tris needed him more anyway.

"Are we following her?" Upton asked.

He stared at his brother, the man who just saved his life. Did he chase Abby, the woman who'd willingly given herself up, or tend to Tris, the brother who'd saved his life?

"Go," he said with a quick nod. "We'll check my arm on the way." And then Tris began shrugging out of his coat. "I'm no stranger to injury and this feels like a graze."

The carriage started as he helped Tris out of the coat. Relief made him limp. It was, in fact, just a graze.

Tris looked down at his arm and then up at his brother. "What does the note say?"

He shook his head. He'd been so certain that he'd save her. But in the end…she'd wanted to be a baroness more than anything else. He didn't want to read the note. Didn't want to see the words.

"Read it," East said. "Now."

His gaze flicked up to his half-brother, the question surely reflected in his eyes. "You've already read it, haven't you?"

"It's not sealed," he said with a casual shrug as though that explained everything.

"What does it say?" The carriage reached the street and picked up speed. But Rush didn't check for Westphal. Instead he stared at East. "Tell me."

Instead of answering, East pointed again. "Read it, and then put your head back on straight while we figure out how we're going to rescue her from Westphal again." When Rush still hesitated, East let out a frustrated sigh. "Trust me."

With a shake of his head, his mouth tightening in irritation, he pulled the sheet out from his breast pocket and started to scan the contents, his breath holding in his chest as the words blurred in front of his eyes.

"What is that?" Upton asked.

He blinked as he looked at the duke, who had bent down. "What?"

The duke lifted another scrap of paper and reached out his uninjured hand. "Is that the sheet from the solicitor?" Tris asked, attempting to sit up straighter.

Rush reached for it, plucking it from Upton's hand. The words jumped out at him, stilling his heart. On it was Westphal's address. "What the bloody hell?"

"What does that one say?" East asked, craning his neck.

"It's the same address Mirabelle gave me all those weeks ago. Abby's."

"Why would the solicitor trying to buy our club have Abby's address in his pocket?"

"I don't know," he answered, fear making his chest tight.

"My lord," the driver called, "their carriage has stopped."

Rush wrenched his gaze out the window just in time to see Westphal pull Abby into the house. Westphal had returned to his London townhouse. Abby would remain in London.

He didn't know precisely how he was going to get her back, but he would. Soon.

CHAPTER NINE

ABBY SAID a silent prayer for small favors. Clarence had been so angry when they'd returned that he'd tossed her in her room and locked the door with hardly a word. She'd attempted to sleep, her body worn and exhausted, but the shot that had been fired still rang in her ears and the sight of Rush falling played over and over in her thoughts. Was he all right?

She'd sacrificed herself specifically so that Rush would not be hurt.

Day had slipped into night, and she gave up any pretense of trying to rest.

Just as the sun set, Clarence's valet delivered a meal to her and more ominously, a dress. She said nothing, not that she expected him to. A recent hire by Clarence, he showed her no allegiance and she'd asked for none.

She stared down at the silk dress with a frown. It was pretty enough, a champagne-colored frock with lace cuffs and embroidery on the bodice.

Was this meant to be her wedding gown? She crossed the room and cracked open the window, allowing the cool night air to fan across her overheated cheeks.

She had to find a way out of here. She'd only agreed to wed

Clarence to spare Rush, and for all she knew, he was injured or worse. Grief made her heavy as her chin sank down toward her chest.

The lock clicked and she tensed, all the stiffness returning to her muscles as she spun toward the door.

Clarence stood in the entry to the room, a sneer pulling at his lip. "The dress arrived."

She gave a quick nod, her hands pressing together, not sure what else to say. Did he expect enthusiasm?

"Should I ask why you agreed to marry me?"

She swallowed down a lump as she searched her mind for an acceptable answer. Somehow, she doubted that he'd like to hear that she'd done it to save another man. She was too practical to be a fool now. "It seemed the right thing to do." *In the moment.*

His mouth twisted. "I suppose that's as good an answer as any."

Clarence stepped into the room, closing the door behind him in a way that made her stomach lurch. She'd never been alone in a bedchamber with him before and the possibilities of what he might do made her back up, her legs pressing to the wall as she clutched the sill of the window.

He stopped halfway across the room, eyeing her warily. Did he think she might jump? Her room on the third floor had a sufficient fall. She held her breath at the idea of it. If he tried to touch her…

"Did he compromise you?"

"I'm sorry?"

"Touch you. Take your maidenhead." He waved his hand in the air as his frown deepened.

"Of course not," she said, her other hand coming to the base of her throat.

"Tell me the truth." Clarence's eyes narrowed. "I'll know. Tomorrow, I'll know."

Tomorrow? Did that mean he wouldn't touch her tonight? Were they to marry tomorrow? That gave her a night to plot an escape. A little hope buoyed her as her mind began searching for a plan. "What is it you want, Clarence?"

He started to move closer and she tensed again, trying and failing to move further back. "I want an obedient wife."

Yes. He would. She didn't look at him nor did she answer, sure whatever she said would only cause the situation to grow worse.

"The only reason this conversation is so...amicable is because you came willingly this morning, but do not mistake me. You are never to see that man again."

She swallowed, her throat tight as she kept her gaze averted.

"Everything will be fine for you provided you are reasonable and rational and listen to what I am saying."

She didn't believe him. She'd willingly given herself over and he'd shot at Rush, who hadn't even been armed. That was not what a man of honor did and so she felt no guilt in lying as she nodded her head in agreement.

Clarence stared at her for several more seconds before he finally turned on his heel and left, locking the door behind him. She let out a long breath as she wilted against the frame of the window.

Which is why she nearly screamed when another voice called up to her. "Abby." She jumped back, fear making her stiff as she swallowed down the surprise that clogged her throat. And then, tentatively, she stepped back toward the window, peeking out.

On the second floor balcony below, she could just make out the glowing ember of a cheroot. "Rush?"

"It's me," he answered, a plume of smoke filling the air. She could just make it out by the small ember that lit the end.

"What are you doing here?" she gasped as she leaned further out to better see him. "Are you all right?"

"I'm fine, sweetheart."

"You're certain? Were you hurt? Do you need tending?"

"No," he said, his voice both reassuring and calm. "I wasn't hurt in the least."

"I'm so relieved," she rushed out, her eyes drifting closed for a second. But then she looked down at him. "What are you doing here?"

"I've been here all day," he answered. Her eyes began to adjust to the darkness and she could just make out his tall frame, leaning against the railing as he looked up at her. "Clarence has this place locked up tight as a drum."

She winced, both regret and relief sliding through her. "You've tried to get in."

"Oh yes," Rush said. "I've even tried climbing up to your window, but the stone façade is too slick for me to make it up to the third floor."

"Oh, Rush." Emotion overwhelmed her to know he'd been trying so hard to free her from Clarence. Did he know that she wished to help him too? "Did you get my note?"

"I did. And I appreciate your attempt to save me." He shifted, his voice smooth and sweet despite his next words. "Though if you'd asked, I'd have told you not to bother. I had Clarence well in hand."

She shook her head, thinking back to her note. "But you needed someone to be your champion. I wanted to be that for you."

He stilled, staring up at her. "Abby," his voice suddenly strained. "How did you know that?"

"I've listened to you, Rush. You've dedicated your life to your family. First to pleasing your father and then to the betterment of your siblings, all while they pursue their own interests."

He shook his head. "Tris was shot today protecting me," he said quietly. "And you sacrificed yourself to what..."

"You want to escape and I would tether you here."

He was silent for so long, she might have thought he'd left except for the burning ember of his cheroot. "And what is it you want, sweetheart?"

What did she want? She wanted him. She wanted her father's love. She wanted her inheritance.

But if she only got one of them... "I'd choose you if I could."

"Not being a baroness?"

What did being a baroness have to do with anything?

RUSH FOUND himself holding his breath. Unwise, considering the smoke he'd just inhaled from his cheroot, and he coughed it out, trying to be quiet.

He'd attempted to reach Abby all day, growing more afraid as time passed without seeing her. Until she'd appeared in the window, opening the glass and seemingly unharmed.

Then he'd breathed a sigh of relief and started climbing up the building. But he'd hit an impasse. He couldn't go any further up and the distance between her window and the balcony had to be fifteen feet. She couldn't come down, either.

And then he'd heard Clarence enter.

He'd known without hesitation that if Clarence attempted to hurt her, Rush would break down the front door and take her away forever.

But the man had left again.

And now he sat with a weight on his chest, waiting for her answer. "A baroness?" she repeated, sounding completely confused.

He winced the slightest bit, glad for the dark as he looked away. "Some women might think that a man with a title, one who isn't a bastard, might be superior." Who was he kidding? Even his own father had held that notion. Why wouldn't she?

But her next words made his heart stop. "Those women would be fools."

"Abby," he breathed out as air rushed from his lungs. Had he had this wrong all along? How could that be? She'd told him that he'd ruined her future. But even East had said that her worries were likely financial. "You don't care about being titled?"

"No," she answered simply. "I care about being safe."

The words made sense and he held them in his chest, wanting to believe them.

"The wedding is tomorrow," she said, quietly enough that he might not have heard except the words made his chest tighten.

"Tell me honestly. The choice is still yours. And in the letter you said..." The letter. It still made him ache.

She'd confessed her deepest feelings and swore that she'd gone

69

with Clarence to save Rush. Twice in a single day, two people had raced to his aid. If he counted East, that was three who'd been helping him.

A man could start to think London wasn't such a bad place to be after all. And all this time, he'd been attempting to escape this life for a new one.

"Choice?" she asked, leaning further out the window. "What choice is that?"

"Him or me? Knowing that I can't give you a title. That you won't get your dowry." His fingers tightened on the railing as she looked down at him, her gaze unreadable in the dark.

"You."

That one word made his chest swell and he stamped out his cheroot, his mind springing into action. "Take the linens from your bed and tie them together."

"What?" she asked, straightening. "Do you want me to climb down?"

"No. I'm going to come up," he answered, new resolve making his spine stiff and straight. "And then we're going to find a way out."

"Are you certain?" she asked, shaking her head. "Is it safe?"

But he didn't answer as a noise caught his ear. Distant voices moving closer and closer still. "This is it," one of them said. "Westphal's."

"Abby," he hissed, looking up at her. "Blow out your candle and close your window. Quickly."

He pressed himself against the brick, blending into the shadows as two men appeared. They began to do as he'd done earlier, testing every window and door until they stopped at the corner of the house.

"Anything open?" one asked.

"No. You?"

"All tight," he said, then gave the corner of the building a small kick as though he might loosen some stone to slip inside.

Rush held still as he listened. Who were these men and what were they doing here?

"Guiltmore isn't going to be pleased," the other one answered.

Guiltmore? Who was that?

"They'll have to leave eventually and when they do…" Both men laughed. But Rush's nostrils flared. Who were these men and what did they want with Westphal and Abby? One of his questions was answered almost immediately.

"What will we do with the baron?" the second one asked.

"Kill 'im. He's of no consequence. It's the girl we need."

"And what does Guiltmore 'ope to do with a girl again?"

"None of your business." The first man gave the second a bit of a shove. "You just worry about snatching her."

"How long will we have to stay here?" the second asked, clearly not the man in charge.

"It takes as long as it takes. Hope your coat is warm, we're staying for the night."

Rush ground his teeth together as the two men disappeared into the shadows. He couldn't make a racket now by climbing in through her window. They were being watched.

He'd have to wait too. Settling in to his spot on the balcony, several minutes passed before he heard the window open again and Abby's soft whisper. "Rush?"

"I'm here," he whispered back. "And I'm not going anywhere."

"Is everything all right?"

"It's fine, sweetheart. But I've got a new plan," he answered. "Get ready tomorrow and go with Westphal like nothing is amiss."

"You want me to marry him?" she asked, her voice growing high and tight.

"The only man you're marrying is me. Now try to get some rest."

"I will." She sighed into the night. "I wish you were up here and instead of down there."

"Don't worry, my love. I'll see you at the church."

CHAPTER TEN

ABBY STOOD in front of the looking glass marveling at how well the dress fit her. How had Clarence managed it?

She'd finally found something he was good at: picking stunning wedding gowns for reluctant brides.

Shaking her head, she crossed to the window and peeked through the curtains. Was Rush out there still? He'd promised that he would be and it made the day easier to face.

She stood straighter as she drew in a fortifying gulp of air and smoothed her loose coiffure, her curls sliding through her fingers.

How would Rush save her? She knew he would. Should she have allowed him to duel? Would they be tucked safely in the Earl of Easton's home right now if he had? She crossed to the window to search for him, but all she could see was the garden below, the branches dancing in the breeze.

She wished that she might have laid eyes on him this morning, but she knew he was out there. And he'd save her. She was sure of it.

Shuddering, she pushed these thoughts away as she returned to her dressing table. Pinning her hair, her thoughts drifted back to Rush. Abby needed to find a way to repay him for all he'd done. Prove to him that she'd fight as hard for him as he did for her. He'd save her today and with any luck, she would be back in a safe home tonight.

Crossing the room, she made her way to the bed to sit and wait. She had no idea what time Clarence would unlock the door. Surely it was the morning since he'd planned a church wedding.

It felt as though she'd sat for hours when the lock finally turned, clicking open. Clarence appeared in the door, staring at her without entering. "It's time."

She gave a quick nod as she stood, then smoothed her skirts and passed by him without touching any part of him. She'd not touch him now or ever, but his hand shot out to wrap about her upper arm. "You'll accept my escort, Abigail. Just as you'll accept me as your husband tonight, and all that the position entails."

A shiver of revulsion slithered down her spine, but she kept her chin high as she tucked her hand in his arm. Rush was out there. Waiting.

He'd said he'd be at the church. Abby would trust him now. Clarence hurried her through the entry and down the steps, then quickly loaded her in the carriage and climbed in behind her.

Was Clarence in a hurry or just worried that Rush might be waiting to steal her back?

"I'm surprised you didn't wish for your mother to be here," she murmured, just trying to fill the awkward silence.

"Never you mind about her," Clarence snapped.

Abby opened her mouth to reply. Clarence had been closely tied to his mother's apron strings as a child. What had changed? But then she closed her lips again, pressing them together. It didn't matter.

Instead, she scanned the street out the window, attempting to remain casual. She'd not want to give Rush's plans away now.

Pressing her hands together to try to keep them from trembling, she drew in a shaky breath.

"What's the matter with you?" Clarence snapped from across the carriage.

"I'm nervous," she answered, meeting his gaze as steadily as she was able. "You're not?"

"No," he replied. "Marrying you is the next necessary step."

How romantic. She looked back out the window. "Step to what?"

"That land your father bequeathed you is the single best piece of real estate in all of the county. Perhaps the country."

She blinked in surprise, her heart jumping in her chest. "What?"

He scowled at her. "You knew your dowry was the property at Upton Falls?"

"Yes, but..." She tapered off. She had no idea the property was successful. Was it possible her father had loved her a bit after all?

"Mayhap it was nothing when he chose it, but now...the crops, the location, it's worth three times any other property in the barony."

She stared in shock. The home on the estate was modest when compared to the others. She'd assumed her father had given her the smallest and least valuable plot.

Why would her father give her such a wonderful gift and not provide her a decent guardian? Not that she could ask him. Even if he were here, they'd never been good at communicating. "Just to be clear, you want to marry me for my land?"

She rarely saw Clarence smile, but he did then. How a man could look less attractive when happy, she had no idea, but he managed the feat, happiness twisting his features into a frightening mask.

"Among other things," he answered and then his gaze slid down her body.

She shrank into the seat as she scanned the street again. Carriages lined the road, but two horsemen caught her eye.

They were odd only in that they were staring directly at Clarence's carriage as they kept pace. Her gaze fixed on them as theirs stared back at the vehicle. "Do you know those men?" she asked, looking at Clarence.

She didn't trust him as a protector any more than she did as a guardian, but she was certain he wanted her to at least make it to the ceremony.

His gaze narrowed as he studied the two horsemen, lifting from his seat and pushing the curtain further back. "Not Lord Smith's men?"

She shook her head. "I've never seen them before."

"They have that rough look like they might be with him." His lip curled. "Dock trash."

She bit the inside of her cheek as words sprang to her lips. How dare Clarence say such things about Rush? She trusted Rush ten times over to protect her, keep her safe. But the argument was pointless and they had a much larger potential problem. Her gaze moved back to the men, who were still staring.

The carriage turned and she lost sight of them both. She craned her neck, trying to catch a glimpse of them as the carriage slowed, rolling to a stop.

"We're here," Clarence said, as a footman swung open the door.

"The church?" she asked, knowing it was a silly question. Where else would they be? Clarence stepped out and then reached back to take her hand as she moved toward him.

She just caught sight of the chapel, the thick, slatted wooden door, propped open as candles burned within.

The scene was lovely and she paused for a single moment. Her real wedding was going to be wonderful. Because one way or the other, she was not marrying Clarence today. Of that, she was certain.

Abby looked at him again. Did she refuse to leave the carriage? Was Rush out there now? Did she go inside? She drew in a deep breath and reached out to take Clarence's hand. She trusted Rush to see her through this. But just as her head cleared the door, a shot rang out, and for the second time in two days, she found herself crouching down, her hands coming to her ears.

In the next moment, the heavy thud of a body falling echoed through her ears before the carriage, door still open, lurched forward again.

She let out a cry as she fell back, the crack of the whip spurring the horses into action.

She tried to keep herself from crashing into the seat in front of her as Rush yelled, "Hold on."

"Rush," she cried, doing as he commanded, reaching for the handle near the door.

But he didn't answer as the vehicle picked up speed. What had just happened? Who had been shot and who had done the shooting? Who had fallen, and most pressing—where were they going?

She held on tightly as she remained huddled by the floor.

———

THEY REACHED Easton's estate like the hounds of hell were following them. Perhaps they were.

Those two men had tailed Westphal and Abby to the church and then one of them had fired at Westphal without warning.

Rush had taken full advantage. The footmen were already off the carriage, he only needed to push the driver from his seat and crack the whip to get the vehicle moving again. However, he'd stolen a baron's carriage. And though it had once again been a rescue, he wasn't certain Westphal would see it that way.

But the men could have followed. He scanned the street as Upton and Easton rushed from the house, both holding pistols in their hands. Some of his tension eased to see them.

"You're back," East called as Rush raised his own pistol, standing on the bench and watching the street again.

He didn't intend to stay for long. "Is my carriage still here?"

"Yes," East said as he came to a halt. "I took Tris home myself in my carriage."

"Was he all right?" he asked, still watching to see if they'd been followed. But his chest tightened to think of his brother.

"Fine. And Gris wrote this morning to say Tris fares as well as can be expected. Grumpy as hell, which Gris thinks is an excellent sign."

Rush gave a quick nod, glad for the update. "Two men staked out Abby's home last night. I overheard them say they worked for a man named Guiltmore."

"Guiltmore?"

"They fired at Westphal, which is how I managed to slip away with his carriage. It will need to be returned to him posthaste." Then he added much more softly, "If he lives." Rush wasn't certain if the baron had been shot or not.

"I'll take it back," Upton said. "How likely is he to shoot me when I arrive?"

Rush gave a small smile to the man that he'd only recently come to know, though found he liked immensely. "He might be mortally wounded. I didn't stop to check."

"And where will you go?" East asked before climbing into the carriage, surely checking on Abby, for which Rush was grateful.

His half-brother stepped back out a moment later, calling for Rush's carriage. Rush jumped down, striding to the door and reaching his hand in for Abby.

Instead, she launched herself out of the vehicle and into his arms. He knew he should remain vigilant but for a moment, he pulled her close, burying his nose in her hair. "I told you I'd come for you."

"I never doubted," she choked into his shoulder as she burrowed deeper into him.

Behind him, East cocked a brow and ushered them back toward the carriage house. Rush carried Abby, not even bothering to pretend at decorum. He wanted her close.

"Thank you," he said to East, not sure how to tell the man he'd avoided for his entire life that he'd been more supportive in the past few days than their father throughout the years before he passed. Someday, he'd find the words.

Perhaps East understood already. He gave Rush a quick nod. "Anytime, brother. Anytime."

Fifteen minutes later, he and Abby set off, having chosen their course. She sat on his left side, several pistols on his right. He was prepared for any circumstance. He hoped.

"Upton Falls, is it?" He looked at her as she jerked her chin in affirmation.

"That's right."

"Why there?" he asked, now they'd left East behind.

She sat next to him, her hands threaded through one of his. "It's mine."

His brows lifted. "Really?"

"Well, it could be. It's my dowry, after all."

"But Clarence controls your dowry."

She nodded. "I have friends in Upton Falls. I'm hoping one of them can help us."

He winced a bit. He hoped so too. Because, as much as she'd chosen him, she clearly held out hopes of capturing her dowry still.

Was she worried he couldn't provide for her? But he forced these thoughts aside. If anyone knew about how complicated her feelings for her father might be, it was him. And so he didn't ask more as they started the journey out of London and to Upton Falls.

It was only a day's ride from the city, but they'd no more made their way over the North Bridge when Abby slumped against him, falling asleep.

He hadn't slept much either on his perch on the balcony, and as he slid his arm about her shoulders, he buried his nose in her hair and breathed her in.

He'd be enough for her. Somehow, some way.

He didn't want to sleep. He needed to remain vigilant but as the carriage swayed, her body warm and soft pressed to his, his eyes began to close.

"Rush?" she asked, her voice sleepy and sweet next to him.

"My love?"

"Should we be going to Gretna Green instead?"

His hand ran over her spine. "We'll stop at Upton Falls and then decide from there."

"That is an excellent plan." She nodded against his chest.

"I'm glad you like it," he whispered against her temple. "And don't worry. I'm going to protect you. I promise. I'll keep you safe and I'll make certain that Westphal never steps near you again."

"I know you will," she said, then lifted her face to stare into his eyes. "But I haven't been able to save you yet. Not really. And I believe it's my turn. Surely our stop will provide some answers."

Save him? What did that mean? And what did he have to do with Upton Falls?

CHAPTER ELEVEN

ABIGAIL WOKE SUDDENLY, aware that the rocking motion of the carriage, which had lulled her to sleep earlier, had stopped.

It was night now, the darkness only accentuating the hard, warm body she was pressed against, the steady beat of Rush's heart under her ear. "Where are we?" Her voice came out slurred from sleep.

"Upton Falls," he answered, pushing back the curtain.

"We're here! How long have I been asleep?"

He chuckled. "Eight hours, give or take?"

"Did you sleep?" she asked, glad the dark covered the heat of her cheeks. She hadn't meant to sleep so long. They had much to discuss, it was just that she'd hardly slept the past few days and the exhaustion had overtaken her. It had helped that she'd been pressed against his hard strength.

"A bit," he answered, shifting to rise off the seat and open the carriage door. "Will the staff know you?"

"Oh yes," she answered with a nod. "This was always my favorite place. The river is near the house and so lovely with a waterfall on the property. My father didn't care for this estate, but he'd bring me here every few years just to check on it, I think."

"Why didn't he like it?" Rush asked, helping her from the carriage.

"I don't know. I always assumed it was because this was the smallest and simplest house in the barony."

Rush stopped, staring up at the estate just visible in the moonlight. "This is small?"

She laughed, taking his hand. "Comparatively."

"I must warn you, since we've discussed moving on to Gretna Green, that the house we'll live in in London is much smaller and—" He paused with a grimace.

"But you took a position outside of London." She sat up, looking at him with worried eyes.

He reached for her face, stroking her chin. "The club will better provide for us."

"But—"

"This is what a man does." His palm cupped her cheek. "He provides. I'll do whatever I have to provide for you."

"But you wanted to leave your family. Your brothers." Her heart was swelling painfully. She appreciated what he was saying so much, but she didn't want him to give up his dreams for her.

"Do you not like Tris? I can understand why. He's a very large pain."

She laughed and it felt so good to do so. "I like your brother."

"You've only met the one and he was on his best behavior." He grimaced as they made their way up the stairs.

She continued to giggle. "I'm sure they're all wonderful. But if you're not taking that other job, then perhaps we can make a future—" But she didn't get to finish.

The door burst open and Roderick, the butler who had been at the property for most of her life, stepped out. "Lady Abigail," he cried with a large smile. "What a surprise."

She returned the gesture as she stepped forward. "Good to see you too, Roderick. This is Lord Smith, my escort."

The butler peered over her shoulder with a slight frown. He surely had a great many questions, but he kept quiet as he showed them inside.

"We'll need dinner," she called over her shoulder. "And send word to Mister Fairfield that I'll need to see him first thing in the morning. Lord Smith will need a room prepared, as will I," she said as she removed her gloves. It was good to be here, the place that had always been the most like her home.

She breathed in the air, always fresh here, and for a moment she closed her eyes.

"Of course, my lady," Roderick answered with a quick bow. "Dinner will be ready shortly."

"You're at home here," Rush said from next to her, his hand subtly brushing her waist.

"I am," she answered with a nod.

"And who is Mister Fairfield?"

She gave him a meaningful glance before she answered. "My father's friend and a solicitor. If anyone understands the particulars of my dowry, then it is him."

Rush's eyes widened in surprise. "That's why you wanted to stop here."

She gave a nod. "I know he forwarded most of the documentation to another solicitor in London, but no one, including my father, has ever explained them to me. I've never liked Clarence, but I somehow assumed that he was being honest with me even if he wasn't particularly kind. But after the duel, the way he acted, I've been wondering…"

Rush drew in a deep breath. "You think he might have lied?"

"It's possible. No one tells a woman my age anything." He held out his hand to her and she slipped her fingers into his, so glad for the touch.

"Regardless of what you find out, know that I will take care of you."

Her heart swelled as she squeezed his fingers tighter. He didn't need to repeat the sentiment. "Rush, I don't doubt it."

"I know you want your dowry. If my father had left me something, I'd want it too."

She did want this place for all those reasons and more, but it was

Rush's entrance into her life that had compelled her to fight. For herself and for him.

The butler appeared once again and Rush let go of her hand as they were ushered into a sitting room. A tray was quickly brought in with snacks and wine.

Several more candles were lit, and Abby sank deeper into the plush chair next to the fire. She'd always loved this room. In the daylight hours, one could see the front drive and the river off to the left with its small bridge that allowed for carriages to pass.

She pointed toward it, tapping Rush with her other hand. "All carriages entering from the road have to cross the bridge."

"I noticed," he said with a glance. "But I appreciate you pointing it out."

"I'll tell the staff to be extra vigilant," she murmured as more food was brought in.

"We're just going to dine here?" Rush asked in the chair across from her.

"Do you mind? I didn't think you'd wish for anything formal after spending the day in the carriage."

"Mind?" he asked with a chuckle. "This is the most comfortable I've been in ages."

"Me too," she answered back. "But I only need to see Mister Fairfield, and then we can decide where to go from here. If nothing else, he'll be able to help us decide."

Rush gave a nod as he helped himself to a piece of kidney pie. "It's a good plan, Abby. Well done."

She sank back in her chair, popping another olive in her mouth. She was glad she'd slept today because she wasn't certain she would tonight.

Their meeting with Fairfield tomorrow would determine the course of the rest of her life.

———

RUSH LOOKED AT ABBY, lounged back in her chair, feet tucked under her, firelight dancing off her flawless skin. She was stunning in London, but here…

She belonged in this place.

He understood why she'd been fighting for Upton Falls. She'd fought for him too when she'd stopped that duel, or she'd tried to. And that mattered.

Perhaps someday, he'd rank as high as Upton Falls. Because for him, somewhere along the way, she'd become more important than anything else. His past with his father, his future with or without his family. Abby was his priority. Period.

Her eyes had fluttered closed, long lashes resting on her cheeks as her head lolled back. He stood, quietly, and removed his coat and cravat.

Then he sat back down to remove his boots.

"What are you doing?" She didn't sound alarmed, just curious.

"Getting comfortable," he answered. "It's been a long few days and this feels like the sort of place we might be able to relax." Granted, he'd likely not sleep much tonight. He'd keep her safe today and always.

She gave him a sleepy smile that nearly melted his insides, filling him with a wistful sort of ache. He wanted all those smiles. But he also wished for a great deal more than just those smiles. "I always felt that way too. In London, all of the *ton* is watching, and even before I was old enough to realize that fact, I just liked the quiet here. The lack of people, the beauty. Room to spread and move and just be."

He leaned forward, hearing his own inner wants said out loud. "I didn't know that was what you wished."

Her eyes widened as she sat up. "Oh. I suppose that's true. My desire for such a life was encapsulated in a specific place."

He looked around, understanding exactly how alike they were. "You never wanted to be a baroness."

"I told you that."

He shook his head. "I'm a bit thick," he said, but he drank in the room realizing that she'd been trying to tell him. "Do you love this place because your father gave it to you as well?"

She shook her head. "I do wish he loved me more. But my affection for Upton Falls is not because he gave it to me. It's just where I'm happiest. I suppose, if I'm honest, him leaving it to me made me hope that he loved me too."

He understood that. "It's a fool's errand to hope for love from a dead father."

She reached out for his hand. "But you do anyway."

He shrugged. "I did. And then I realized how ridiculous an endeavor it was to try and please a dead man. One who'd hardly paid me mind when he was alive. One who'd barely even provided for us." He shook his head. "But why would I be angry at my brothers too? I'm only just realizing that I have been."

She threaded her fingers through his. "If I were to guess…"

"Please do."

"They remind you of him."

His brow crinkled. "How so?"

"Well, you have devoted your whole life to their betterment, and they've been off doing what they please for their own personal gain."

"Christ," he muttered, sitting up straighter, the truth like a punch in the gut. "I am angry at them for exactly that."

Her fingers threaded through his. "I understand."

"Upton Falls is exactly how I pictured the property I was going to live on as estate manager. The place where I was going to be the person I wanted to be."

"I think it's all right for them to want things for themselves, just as it's completely understandable that you would want the same. I know I already said it, but once we're married, you can still take the position if you'd like."

He shrugged. Abby was not meant to be an estate manager's wife. And her care was his priority now. "I'm ready to forgive my brothers and continue to work with my family. It offers the most potential."

She bit her lip as she stared at him. "You're certain? I don't blame you for being angry at your father. He was selfish at your expense, and I'd be angry as well if I were you."

"And my brothers? Should I still be angry at them?"

She shook her head. "I don't know. I've only met Tris but..."

With startling clarity, he saw the situation exactly as she'd described it. "Abby."

"Yes?" She gave him another dazzling smile. The sort that lit the dark places inside him and hit him like another punch. He loved this woman so much.

"My brothers. They would put their priorities aside for me when I need them."

"And you for them," she whispered. "At least Tris. I'm excited to meet the rest of them. I didn't have siblings. Having a big family close by seems wonderful."

He slid from his seat, keeping her hand in his as his knees landed on the floor next to her chair. "Love."

"Yes?" Her gaze searched his as his free hand trailed over her knee, tracing her leg up to her hip.

"I want you to know"—his voice had taken on a roughness that he barely recognized—"that I won't let anyone hurt you. Not Clarence Westphal, not whoever those men were. I can't promise you Upton Falls, I'm sorry. But I can swear to that."

She skimmed her free hand along his jaw and into his hair, combing the strands back. "Whatever you choose to do in the future, we'll make a happy home together, Rush. I'm sure of it. And we'll do it together." Her gaze held his as she said the words and his chest swelled with all the emotions that coursed through him.

Leaning closer, he stopped when his face was just a few inches from hers. "I love you."

"I love you too," she answered, the words crashing over him a second before he captured her mouth with his own.

CHAPTER TWELVE

THE FEEL of his Rush's mouth on hers made Abby breathless with want. He was so strong, and despite the danger that had swirled about them, she'd never felt safer or more loved in her life.

She understood now what she'd been needing all this time and how she received it as well. She might keep Upton Falls, she might lose this place. But her home was with Rush now and he was the part worth fighting for.

She held him close, wrapping her hands about his neck as the kiss deepened and lengthened, his tongue sweeping into her mouth, their tongues tangling together.

His chest touched hers, their mouths locked together, but as the kiss went on, Abby had the vague sensation that she needed to be closer still.

Rush clearly understood what she needed because, without breaking the kiss, he stood, pulling her with him, their bodies coming together as they stood.

She gasped at the touch, the feel of their bellies, hips, and thighs coming together so delicious and satisfying that the ache between her legs throbbed with need.

She squirmed against him, trying to relieve it with pressure as one of Rush's hands slid down to her behind, and squeezing, he pulled their hips even more tightly together, intensifying the need building inside her.

"Rush," she gasped. "Please."

Rather than answer with words, he pulled her down toward the floor, laying her out in front of the fire, his body coming on top of hers.

Her thighs naturally parted, creating a cradle for him between her legs.

And as the hardness of him pushed into her soft core, she moaned with a deep satisfaction, her fingers winding into his hair and tugging at the strands.

He rumbled against her lips before he slid his mouth along her jaw, kissing a trail down her neck and over her collarbone.

Her wedding gown boasted a square neckline that revealed a fair bit of décolletage, a fact that Rush took full advantage of as he kissed down her chest and over the top of her breasts.

She tugged even harder on the thick stands of his hair, until he pulled one of her breasts out of the dress, his tongue flicking out to tease the nipple a moment before his whole mouth covered it, sucking the puckered flesh between his lips.

She moaned, arching her back. Never had she imagined such pleasure and her legs wrapped about the back of his thighs, searching for more.

And he gave it. Even as he continued to work her nipple, he pushed up her skirts until they were gathered about her waist. His hand skimmed up her thigh past her stockings until he'd reached her hot core and then he brushed his fingertips down her slit.

The sensation that rocked through her made every part of her body tighten as she cried out, her hips rocking into the touch.

He made another teasing pass, making her both hot and needy. With everything he gave, she only wished for more.

And then his fingers made another pass, more purposeful, increasing the pressure. She turned her head to the side as she bit at her lip, pleasure radiating out from her core.

His mouth left her breast as he moved lower, his shoulders settling between her thighs.

For a moment she tensed, wondering what he might do next, but her question was quickly answered. As his fingers slid through her folds, his tongue followed their trail, sliding through her most intimate flesh in a way that sent the most delicious heat spiraling through her.

Her hands were still in his hair and instinct demanded that she pull him closer, increasing the pressure as he worked her body, stoking the passion until she was certain she'd combust with need.

He slid one of his fingers into her channel, the sensation almost more than she could bear as sparks lit behind her eyes.

And finally, when she was sure she could not stand another moment, her pleasure broke, a cry falling from her lips as she came undone.

Her body went limp as her fingers finally relaxed, combing through his hair as he climbed back up her body.

She swept her hands down his neck and then around to his face even as his mouth dropped to hers, his weight pressing into hers once again.

That's when she felt the bulge, rock hard in his breeches.

She slid a hand down his side and, reaching between their bodies, cupped the length of his manhood, feeling it in her palm.

"Abby," he groaned, low and deep, his voice strained with his own want.

He had the same urge she had, only hers had been filled. And she knew this was another way in which she could and should give to him.

She kept exploring him, gliding her fingers over the fabric covering his length, his hips flexing to thrust against the friction of her hand. "Tell me what to do," she whispered against his mouth. "I want to please you."

He reared up, pulling at the buttons of his breeches as she reached to help him, until they'd wrestled the tight garment over his hips, his manhood springing forward into her hand. She drew in a breath to see it jutting forward and he let out a guttural chuckle. "I'm not nearly as pretty as you."

She shook her head. "It's not that. I just... I've wondered for so long. And now..." She reached out again, letting her fingers trail over his velvety skin. He was both soft and hard, and as she brushed the pad of her thumb over the tip, he sucked in a breath. Falling to one side, he rolled onto his back and she went with him, touching him until he wrapped his fingers around hers, helping her to work his flesh up and down.

She opened her eyes wider, fascination making her draw closer.

This strong, powerful man was at her mercy in this moment, his body begging for the pleasure she could give. She stroked him faster, reveling in the power of it but also the beauty, the bond that drew them together.

And when he was so tense he seemed as though he might snap from it, he let out a groan, seed spilling from his manhood.

Without a word, he pulled her even closer, settling her into the crook of his body, the fire at her back.

She sank willingly into him, and despite being tangled on the floor, she wasn't certain she'd ever been more comfortable.

That was her last thought before she drifted off to sleep.

———

RUSH WAITED until Abby had fallen into a deep sleep before he moved. He straightened her skirt and then settled her on the settee. Then he straightened his own clothes and stoked the fire before he went in search of the staff.

He found the butler in the pantry. "Good evening," he said as he entered. "My apologies for disturbing you, Roderick."

The man gave him a short bow, his gaze curious. "Not at all, my lord."

"I know you said that the staff would be on the lookout, but would it be too much trouble to have a few footmen or stable hands patrolling the grounds throughout the night?"

The man gave him another bow. "Of course. Consider it done." Roderick started to turn but then looked back at Rush. "My lord, may I ask a question?"

He gave a quick nod.

"Who is Lady Abigail in danger from that you are so concerned?"

Rush considered his answer as he stroked his chin. How did he begin to explain? "Well, for starters, her guardian."

Roderick blinked in surprise. "Lord Pembly?"

"Pembly? Who is that?" He took a step closer. "Her guardian is the new Baron Westphal."

Roderick's face paled. "That can't be."

"It is."

Roderick shook his head. "Forgive me, but I served at the very meeting where Lady Abigail's father, the former baron, had the documents drawn up that declared his estranged brother-in-law, Lord Pembly, Abigail's guardian."

Surprise rocked through him. "Estranged?"

Roderick shook his head, as though he didn't wish to say more. "It's not my place to share more, but if you're meeting with Mister Fairfield tomorrow, he can surely provide the details I cannot."

Rush gave a quick nod as the other man turned to execute the instructions. He returned to the sitting room where Abby slept and watched her as he leaned against the mantel.

What would Abby think of this new development? Was the man better or worse than Westphal? And how had Westphal gained control of Abby if he wasn't her guardian?

And then there were the other attackers. And Guiltmore... Who was that?

Would they catch up to them before Rush had figured any of this out?

He cursed softly under his breath. Hopefully, Fairfield would be able to shed light on all of this.

Finally, near dawn, he sat in one of the chairs, dozing as he waited for Abby to wake. Some sleep would help him to think and he needed all of his faculties now.

As the sun rose in the sky, he woke when she stirred, her soft sighs the first indication that she was no longer asleep.

He opened his eyes to find her looking at him. "We're not on the floor anymore."

He smiled at her. "I thought you'd be more comfortable on the settee."

"Perhaps." She sat up and stretched, her slender arms reaching up over her head as her hair once again tumbled from their pins. Very soon he was going to hold all that hair in his hands, run his fingers through it, watch it fan out on his chest. "But I liked being next to you."

He stood, crossing the room to the settee and scooping her up before he sat again, settling her in his lap.

She giggled as she wound her arms about his neck. "You know, this house has six bedrooms. We could have used one of them."

That made him laugh too as he buried his nose in her neck. "I wanted to keep an eye on the drive."

Pulling away, she searched his face. "Were you awake all night?"

"I slept enough." He could see the worry clouding her gaze and he brushed his knuckles over her cheek. "And I learned something very interesting from Roderick."

"What did you learn? And when did you talk to Roderick?"

"After you fell asleep," he answered.

"He was still up?" Her gaze skittered to the door. "Do you think he knows what we were doing in here?"

Rush shrugged. "We didn't have a great many servants. I'm not adept at knowing their habits."

She nodded, catching her lip between her teeth. Gently, he cupped her chin to bring her gaze back to his. How would she feel to know that Clarence had tricked her once again? His own gut twisted on her behalf. "But listen. I've important news."

"What is it?"

"Your father did not leave you to Westphal. He assigned your uncle as guardian."

Her mouth fell open as she stared at him. "What?"

"Pembly."

"But…" She shook her head. "We didn't speak to my aunt or uncle after my mother's death. Not once."

"Your father must have had a change of heart."

Tears welled in her eyes as she tightened her hold about his neck. "Why didn't he tell me? And why did the solicitor in London insist that Westphal was my guardian? I spent three months alone in that house in mourning while I waited for Westphal to return from France."

"You waited three months for Westphal to claim his barony?"

She nodded. "Yes. Why?"

"And he knew he was the heir?"

"Of course," she answered, her brow crinkling. "It was obvious my father would not remarry or have more children."

How had he never asked these questions before? "Why?"

"My mother died in childbirth with their second child," Abby answered softly. "I never asked, and he never said, but I heard it whispered by one of the maids that the baby had been a boy."

He winced in sympathy. He could see how that might break a man. A wife was his to protect. But despite his sympathy, he attempted to focus on the issue at hand, and a nagging thread that was dangling in his thoughts. "And you'd met your cousin before?"

"I mean, my father and I hadn't seen him and his mother since Clarence and I were children. My father ceased socializing after my mother died."

There was something odd here. Yet another solicitor that was somehow involved and an heir that took a great deal of time to arrive. Then there were the men whose conversation he'd overheard where they'd been told they could dispose of a baron. Most petty criminals would never be so knowingly callous with the aristocracy. It meant certain death for them.

He looked at Abby's inquisitive gaze and asked the only other question he could think of. "And you're certain that Westphal is the boy you knew?"

She blinked in surprise. "Well. He had the same spoiled manner, I'll give him that. But…" She shook her head. "I did find it odd that his mother never came to visit and he never mentioned her. She doted on her son when he was a child."

His jaw clenched as he considered this detail. "I'm beginning to form a theory."

CHAPTER THIRTEEN

ABBY AND RUSH sat in the carriage, both her hands wrapped around one of his as it rested in her lap. She leaned over, placing her cheek on his shoulder.

They were on their way to see Fairfield and then after that, their destination was anyone's guess.

She wasn't a fool, she understood what Rush had been asking. Was Westphal actually who he claimed to be?

Abby had no idea. She'd not questioned his identity before today, but once Rush had asked, her mind had begun to spin. How Clarence never mentioned a single childhood memory they might have shared before her mother's death. How he didn't speak of his mother, either.

Then there was the absolute insistence they marry. Her father had six properties, all of them entailed, with the exception of Upton Falls. Why was is it so important to him to retain this one? He'd claimed it was the most profitable, but still, did it really produce that much more then all the rest?

And what of all the lies?

She drew in a shuddering breath, trying to still all her racing thoughts. How many of her questions would her father's friend and solicitor be able to answer?

The carriage ambled over a stone bridge, entering the village that bordered the estate. Roderick had informed her that she'd be visiting Fairfield's home rather than his office, which in and of itself was curious.

He rarely saw clients in his home, not even her father. Unless, of course, they were making a social call. But since her father did so little of that, and they came to Upton Falls rarely, Abby could only remember being in his home a single time.

The carriage pulled up in front of the stately home on the outskirts of the village, its stone façade accentuated by well-maintained flower boxes. And yet, at nearly ten in the morning, the shutters had yet to be opened.

Rush stepped out of the carriage, handing her out as well, and they approached the door, Rush lifting his hand to the knocker.

Mrs. Fairfield quickly answered the door, her face as kind as ever, if older, and she ushered Abby and Rush into the front sitting room. "So good to see you."

"And you as well," Abby answered with a warm smile. "I'd like to introduce my fiancé, Lord Smith."

"A pleasure," Mrs. Fairfield said, but her gaze grew guarded as she looked back at Abby. "I must also give my apologies, dear," the woman clucked as she gestured for them both to sit. Crossing the room, she carried over a tea service and poured each a cup of tea.

"For what?" Abby asked, holding her cup of steaming tea as she watched the other woman, genuinely confused.

Mrs. Fairfield set down the pot of steeped tea, her gaze earnest as she answered, "If the circumstances were different, we would have come to London. Collected you and seen you safely guarded..." The woman's hands fluttered before they pressed together. "I'm so sorry we didn't. It's just that—"

"It's not your fault, darling. It's mine." Mr. Fairfield said from the doorway. Abby stood, instantly understanding.

Thin and drawn, the man looked ill. He was dressed just as she remembered him, but the clothes hung loosely off his frame, his hair was far thinner, his skin waxy and pale. "Mister Fairfield," she said, her breath catching. "My sincere apologies for bothering you."

"Not at all," he said as he entered, quickly sinking down into the chair near the fire. Mrs. Fairfield poured him a cup of tea as well, and he gratefully drank it. "I'm glad you're here. I wish we'd been able to settle all of this sooner."

Her chest tightened to think of how sick this man might be. "Thank you for seeing me."

He gave a quick nod. And then he sank further into his seat. "Tell me everything."

Swallowing, she began with the death of her father, the fact that she had no knowledge of the arrangements, the arrival of Westphal three months later, and his plans for their marriage.

Rush added the occasional detail, including how the man had struck her and how he'd felt compelled to intercede.

Mr. Fairfield had looked at Rush then, his head tipping ever so slightly to one side. "And your intentions toward Lady Abigail?"

"Marriage."

"Forgive me, my lord, but how do I know that you're not simply after her dowry?"

Rush coughed, quickly covering it with a hand as he sat up straighter. "Until a half hour ago, I didn't even think there would be one. It seemed well in Westphal's hands."

"Apologies for asking but I needed to be certain." And then Mr. Fairfield cleared his throat. "Whether or not Westphal is an impostor, I can't say. But I do know that it doesn't matter."

"Why not?" Abigail asked, excitement beginning to spread through her.

"He was never your guardian, nor did he ever have control of Upton Falls. That was designated to your uncle, who is deceased, which means it fell to his ne'er-do-well son, who has not responded to a single one of my letters."

Her eyes widened. "So he is responsible for my dowry?"

"As your solicitor, I should inform you that on your twenty-fifth birthday, the property automatically reverts to you. I will send him another letter, inform him of your impending marriage, and ask him to sign over the rights to you early. Normally, with your marriage, the property would revert to your husband."

Rush coughed again, this time barely disguising his shock. "Abby doesn't keep her inheritance when we wed?"

"Not under British law. No. A guardian would work to secure some percentage for her, but as hers has been unreachable, that isn't an option."

"I will act as steward of the property. No more," Rush said with a shake of his head. But then he looked at Abby. "Though we shall have to save enough money that each child gets a percentage. I know you would want it to stay in the family, but I would want to provide for each of our children's futures."

Her heart jumped in her throat. How could one man be that wonderful?

———

RUSH WATCHED Abby's mouth tremble, her large eyes the slightest bit watery as she looked at him. Had he upset her?

But then she held out her hand to him, her fingers pressing into his. "Rush." Her voice was so soft that he barely heard it.

"Yes, love?"

"Upton Falls," she whispered, her hand shaking in his. "I was going to make your dreams come true."

"What?" he asked, searching her face as he leaned closer.

"Your independence. Upton Falls is your chance. It's...I...I'm going to save you the way you have me."

He sat back in the chair, shock coursing through him. Was she attempting to tell him that she was going to marry him and give him an entire estate?

She looked every inch the beauty next to him, her blue eyes crinkling at the corners as they held his. "Abby," he said, at a loss for words. She had come here not for herself but for him. His heart swelled in his chest. He was her soldier. Now and forever. But she—she'd been fighting for him too.

"You said you wanted to manage another property, but we could run Upton Falls together. I know you can keep the books and there would be plenty of opportunity for you to be outside, to be busy and active—"

He cut her off by leaning over to kiss her quiet. He loved this woman so much. The idea that they'd live at Upton Falls forever, that he'd just spent the first night of his future here, filled him with so much gratitude he could do little else besides touch her.

Mrs. Fairfield gasped as Mr. Fairfield cleared his throat. Right. They had witnesses.

Slowly, he leaned back, still holding her hand in his. "You're right. Upton Falls would be a dream come true. To work the land, to live here." He squeezed her fingers. "And the fact you care enough to make that happen for me is more than I deserve."

She shook her head, but he didn't let her finish.

"But you will retain ownership." He looked at Mr. Fairfield. "We'll need some time to work out the details of how we provide for our future children and how the inheritance will work."

Mr. Fairfield gave him a large smile, some color returning to his face. "I have some suggestions."

Rush gave a quick nod.

"I will also write to her guardian. With luck, you should be able to marry in the next few months."

That made Rush rumble out his dissatisfaction. "*Months* is unacceptable."

"Is a child on the way?" Mrs. Fairfield asked and then began to blush.

"No," they both answered simultaneously. Color infused Abby's cheeks as well as she dipped her chin in embarrassment. He placed an arm behind her on the back of the settee. He'd provide whatever comfort he could.

"But we left London with the Duke of Upton and the Earl of Easton attempting to locate the solicitor who has been terrorizing my business while also dealing with Westphal, and I'd like to make their job as easy as possible by ensuring Abby's safety. If we don't marry here, we'd thought to continue north to Gretna Green. But either way, we will be wed within the week."

He understood that the man wanted to preserve Abby's legacy and Rush would never deny Abby her inheritance. When they returned, he'd sign whatever was necessary, but he'd keep her safe just as he'd promised. Nothing was more important than that.

Mr. Fairfield's jaw tightened as he rubbed at it. "I see your point." He stood then and crossed to a desk that sat in the corner. Pulling out paper and an inkwell, he began to scratch the quill across the paper.

When he'd finished, he waved Rush over to the desk.

Rush read down the page, seeing that it was a temporary contract and a proposed negotiation with her guardian. The suggested terms would include ten thousand pounds per child born into the match. It made several other stipulations, including one that explained the retention of property should either of them perish. Rush's brows lifted. "This is remarkably thorough."

Mr. Fairfield looked to his wife. "I've drafted a similar document before." Then he turned back to Rush. "Do you agree?"

He gave a short nod. It was more than fair. He signed the bottom and waved Abby over, quickly explaining each of the stipulations.

"Are you certain?" she asked as his hand came to the small of her back.

"More than certain," he whispered close to her ear, her scent filling his nostrils as he drank her in. How had he ever doubted that his future was with this woman? "This is the answer to both our prayers. You get the home you always wanted, and I get the life I've always craved." And he'd be close enough to London to continue to help his family in any way they required.

Her eyes grew watery again as she put pen to paper and signed her name.

Mr. Fairfield slumped back in his chair. "Good. Now, Missus Fairfield, would you please take this young couple over to Father Mulcahy? I know that no banns have been posted, but if you explain and agree to act as witness, my hunch is that he'll see them wed for the right amount of coin."

Abigail started, her chin turning up to him again. "Married? Today?"

He pulled her close. "Today is a fine day for a wedding."

CHAPTER FOURTEEN

AN HOUR LATER, Abby stood just outside the church, Rush within. The late morning sun shone down on her as Roderick stood at her side.

"Did you ever think you'd be witness at my wedding?" she asked as she stood next to him.

The older man gave her a kind smile. Still in uniform, he bowed. "I am honored, my lady."

She drew in a shaky breath. "Thank you very much. I greatly appreciate your support. I just..." She paused for a moment, collecting her thoughts. "I didn't expect this all to happen quite so quickly."

Roderick nodded. "It is odd how life moves so fast at critical times."

She considered those words as she peered into the church. Was it just yesterday she'd wondered what her real wedding day might be like? Here she stood, one day later, in her favorite place in the world. Her inheritance was intact and she was marrying the man with whom she'd fallen in love. Her chest grew tight with emotion to know all her dreams were hers to keep. "That does seem to be true."

Roderick shifted. "And Mister Fairfield approves of the match?"

She blinked in surprise at the concern in the other man's voice. "He does. It was his idea we wed today."

"And Upton Falls?"

She understood. He was concerned about his position. "Will remain in my name. And become our full-time residence."

Roderick gave a quick nod. "Good. Your father would approve."

"My father?" she asked. Of course, Roderick knew him. Her father had been his employer. But still, it was odd to have this conversation. To consider him from Roderick's perspective.

But this was a day for oddities. She and the butler had never discussed the past, nor had she imagined that Roderick would also be the man to escort her down the aisle at her wedding.

Did she ask what he thought of all this? Or how much he knew about what her father would like or dislike? About why the man who should have loved her had always been so distant?

"He was never the same after your mother's death."

"How so?" she asked, her heart climbing up into her throat.

Roderick turned to look at her. "I've never seen a more significant change in a person. He seemed to live a half life after her death. Before she passed, he had been so joyful. So strong. And their presence together, your mother and father, had filled Upton Falls with such happiness."

She had a difficult time even picturing that. Her father had always been the reserved, withdrawn man she had grown up with. Had her parents been a love match? Why had that love never extended to herself?

"Unless he was different when away from Upton Falls, but I doubt it. They had a connection, your parents."

She shook her head. "I can't even imagine. He was always so cold."

"Was he?" Roderick winced. "I'm sorry for you and sorry that you weren't here more often."

"I never understood why he didn't like this place, but then again, there is little I did understand when it came to him."

Roderick pulled at the lapels of his coat, shifting next to her. "This was your mother's house."

She gasped in a breath. "It was?"

Roderick nodded. "It was her dowry as well, which is why it isn't

entailed." Then he leaned a bit closer. "She loved it here and you spent a great deal of the first part of your life here."

Though her mother had died when she three, Abby had only the vaguest memories of her.

"You look like her, you know. It's almost uncanny," Roderick added. "Raising you must have been difficult for him."

Her breath hitched as she finally understood something that had plagued her entire life. Her eyes fluttered closed as she thought about all the love she'd wished for as a child.

"All this time, I thought he didn't love me," she confessed as her chin sank into her chest.

"I'm certain he did." It was an exceedingly kind thing for Roderick to say.

She lifted her chin to look over at Roderick. He'd answered so many of her questions, ones she'd thought never to have answered, as gratitude swelled in her chest.

He smiled at her, seeming to understand, as Mrs. Fairfield shuffled down the aisle toward them, waving them both forward. "We're ready for you, dear."

Abby smiled at the other woman as Mrs. Fairfield beamed back. She was so glad that Roderick had told her all that he had. Somehow, it helped to clear her heart as she lifted her skirts to climb the stairs into the church.

She'd marry today with a clear heart and mind.

They moved from the sunlight into the much dimmer interior of the church, her eyes taking a few moments to adjust, the candles flickering from the altar and along the aisle.

She breathed in the scent of incense as her eyes adjusted and she saw Rush at the altar.

Her breath caught to see him so tall, dark, and handsome. His hands were folded in front of him as his gaze caught and held hers.

She loved this man with all her heart. And he loved her back.

He reached out his hand to her, his fingers grasping hers as she took the last two steps to reach his side.

He turned with her so they both faced the front.

"Shall be begin?" the vicar asked with a smile.

At Rush's nod, the ceremony began.

ABBY'S FINGERS in his were the anchor that held Rush through the ceremony that made them husband and wife. He'd never expected to marry, but now that he was here, there was no other path he would choose. This woman belonged at his side and as he held her hands in his, the bond between them strengthened. An unbreakable tie that no one could pull asunder.

The words floated past him, but her touch was solid and real as he agreed to have and to hold her until death did them part.

The promises he made echoed in his heart.

He'd give her all he had and more. And when their lips came together to seal their bond, he closed his eyes, just breathing her in.

This was his woman. His wife.

His to protect, to love, to provide for. This was the life he'd craved outside of his family.

They made their way back to Upton Falls, sharing a small meal that was too quiet for the moment they'd just shared. "I'm sorry we have no family here," he said to her as he watched her eat a delicate jam pastry.

She shook her head. "I'm used to the quiet. Every occasion was like this for me as a child. But it must be difficult for you to not have any of your siblings here."

He blinked back his surprise. It was. He wished his brothers and sisters had shared this moment with them. "How did you know?"

"Your brother stepped in front of a bullet for you. You came to my aid because Mirabelle asked. You work in a business that provides for all of them." She leaned forward, her eyes shining as she whispered, "I've never in my life known someone as quietly giving as you, Rush. I am so lucky..." Her words tapered off, her cheeks growing bright pink, but her message was clear.

"I am lucky too, Abby." He stood then, crossing the dining room to stand next to her. "I've never imagined that a wife would be so intent on making my wishes a reality." And then he reached for her hand, pulling her up from her chair.

She came willingly, her eyes still looking troubled. "After all that Roderick told me about my father, I feel at peace with his memory."

He nodded. She'd told him all about the conversation on their return from the village. "I'm glad."

"But how," she asked, wrapping an arm about his shoulders, "are we going to find that same closure for you?"

He shook his head. "We won't."

"But…" She searched his face.

"My father was a selfish man who hurt all of his children with his carelessness. I'm never going to change that. But I have realized that my siblings, we're not like him. I can find my future and help them with theirs, content to know I will never be as selfish as he was."

Her other arm came about his neck, her body pressing to his as she lifted up, placing a soft kiss on his lips. "That is wonderful."

And then she kissed him again.

She tasted of strawberry jam and sweet promises as he tilted her mouth open and swept his tongue between her lips.

Her tongue met his, fire coursing through him with the touch. Wrapping his arms just below her behind, he lifted her up, and then started out of the dining room and up the stairs to the waiting bedroom.

He started to turn into one when she lifted her head and laughed. "Wrong one."

His brows lifted. "Which room is ours?"

She pointed to the left and he pivoted with her still in his arms. The door was open and he strode through it, stopping only to unwrap one arm long enough to swing the heavy door shut.

Before him stood a large, spacious room with a four-post bed draped in heavy velvet curtains. The room boasted several windows overlooking the front of the house and he quirked a brow as he looked up at her. "I could have watched the drive from here last night."

She laughed then, a hand trailing over his jaw as she nodded. "I didn't want to tell you after the way you slept in that chair."

He shook his head. He'd slept in plenty of chairs in his day and a fair number of narrow cots. What would take some adjusting was the bed that stood against the far wall of this room. The elegance of it was like nothing he'd ever imagined would be his.

"I want to unpin your hair," he said, his voice hoarse and rough with his want but also with his emotions.

She sighed out her acceptance as he slowly set her down, her body sliding along his until her feet touched the floor. And then she unwound her arms from his neck to take one of his hands in hers as she moved to the dressing table in one corner. Sitting down, she lifted her arms to her head, pushing her breasts out in the process, and slowly began to pull the pins from her thick tresses.

He stood watching, entranced by the femininity of the act as her thick tresses began to cascade down her back.

But then he stepped over to help.

CHAPTER FIFTEEN

ABBY DREW in a quick breath as Rush's fingers worked into her hair. They were surprisingly gentle considering the size of his hands.

Carefully, he pulled several pins from her coiffure, freeing the strands as he also massaged her scalp.

She relaxed into the touch, knowing the tingling pleasure his caress caused would soon build into something far less leisurely, but she'd enjoy all of the touches and every sensation they brought.

She tipped her head back, sinking deeper into his hand as the last pin was removed and both his hands now cradled her head, his fingertips rubbing small circles all along her scalp.

And then he leaned over to place a soft kiss on her forehead.

She reached for his forearms, wrapping her hands around them, so solid, as he kissed a trail down her cheek to her jaw.

And then his fingers began to comb though her hair.

"Rush," she groaned with pleasure.

"Come," he answered as he helped her up from the chair, and led her over to the bed. She followed, though much of her tension returned as they made their way to the bed.

She wasn't afraid of Rush. Or even of intimacy, but they'd become man and wife and she knew that there would be some pain involved.

"Relax," he whispered as he shrugged off his coat and then began to undo the tiny row of buttons on the back of her gown. "We've got all day." He brushed her hair over her shoulder as he kept working the buttons until her dress slumped forward.

"All day?" she asked, looking over her shoulder. Did he mean to spend all day in bed?

But he only gave her that charming smile. "I think I shall start by rubbing your back."

Her brows drew together. They'd been intimate last night. She had some knowledge here. "Even I know that's not how a woman becomes a wife."

He chuckled, but as he leaned close, his breath tickled her ear. "That is precisely how a woman becomes a wife. A wife should be treasured. Loved. Cared for. And that is what I intend to do to for you."

"Oh," she breathed as her corset fell away.

He helped her onto the bed, and she slid down, lying on her stomach, her cheek resting on her folded hands as he unlaced her shoes and then slid them off her feet.

He skimmed his hands up her stockinged legs, over her camisole, and around her hips, until they met in the small of her back.

Gently, his hands worked all up and down her back and shoulders as every bit of tension leaked from her body. Months she'd been holding it in, but her eyes drifted closed as he worked some magic over her.

The changing of his touch was so subtle at first, she hardly noticed. First his hand dipped lower, closer to her behind, and then back over her hips and then up her sides, close to her breasts.

Her eyes fluttered open again as she twisted her neck to look at him. "I'm not sure I could move if I had to, I'm so relaxed."

He laughed as his middle finger traced the outer edge of her breast. "Then I've done my job."

He kissed her neck then, once again trailing a hand through her hair.

"Do you think you'll like living here?" she asked as she shyly looked over her shoulder at him again.

His hands stopped as he gave her an easy smile. "I'm going to love it, Abby."

She squirmed around them, wiggling under him until she'd worked her way over onto her back. Looking up into his face, she touched his cheek. "You're certain?"

"I'm certain."

He leaned down then, capturing her lips with his. This time, she didn't feel an ounce of fear as she wrapped her arms about his neck.

Their tongues came together, their lips moving as one as his body came down fully on top of hers.

His legs were still on either side of hers, caging her in his embrace, but she'd never felt more protected as his weight settled over hers.

Sliding her fingers over his neck, she traced the muscles of his back until she reached the waist of his breeches and then she began to tug the shirt, untucking the hem until it came loose so that she could pull the fabric over his head.

He reared up, allowing her to remove the clothing, all the while exposing the rippling muscles of his chest.

Her tongue darted out to lick her lips. In the early afternoon light she could see every delicious detail, which was exciting but it also meant… "Perhaps we should wait until later," she whispered, her eyes drinking in every detail of his bare skin. The way the muscles rippled down to his narrow waist.

"Now. Later," he said as he grasped her shoulder with one hand and waist with the other, helping her down once again. "The answer to both is yes."

"But," she said as his lips teased that spot just behind her ear, "you'll see everything."

In answer, he slid off her down the bed where he reached under her chemise, untying her stockings. "I'm very much looking forward to that."

She shook her head. "But what if…" How did she ask the question?

No one had ever loved her. Not like he did. What if he didn't like what he saw and then he stopped...

He slowly rolled first one stocking down her leg and then lifted the other to do the same. "I'm going to love the sight of you naked as much as I love you."

"How can you be so sure?" she whispered as heat filled her cheeks.

In answer, he stood, shucking his boots and stockings. He was in nothing but his breeches as he crossed his arms over his chest and looked down at her. "Loving someone means you love all of them, Abby. You don't pick and choose. That's what I'm learning." He started to climb up her body once again. "So...even if you're less than perfect, which I very much doubt, you can trust me to love you anyway."

She worried her lower lip. "Promise?"

"I promise." And then his lips came down over hers once again.

———

Rush had been moving so slowly because he wanted Abby to be comfortable and relaxed. Happy even.

But need was building inside him, creating a frenzy that took every ounce of his control to hold back.

How could Abby be worried that he wouldn't approve? She was the most gorgeous creature he'd ever beheld. And as the hem of her chemise crept up her thighs, exposing more of her shapely legs, it only confirmed what he knew...this woman was perfect.

Unable to help himself, he kissed a trail up her leg, following the hem. He heard her rush of breath, watched the rapid rise and fall of her chest as thighs parted to accommodate him, her modesty lost in the pleasure.

He didn't hesitate. As the fabric cleared her mound, he brushed a thumb along her seam and then followed with a definite swipe of his tongue.

She shuddered and moaned, spreading her legs wider as he worked her needy flesh with his tongue, her hips moving with him as she chased the pleasure surely building inside her.

She threaded her fingers into his hair, pulling him even closer as he slid a finger into the channel, groaning at the silkiness of her flesh, the tight wetness that gripped him as she moaned out his name. "Rush."

He groaned too, his body throbbing for more. But he kept up the rhythm, feeling as she grew more frantic, closer and closer until finally she fell over the edge of her pleasure, crying out again.

He shot up, yanking at the buttons of his breeches to undo them, and tugged the tight fabric down over his hips.

Taking several deep breaths to slow his racing body, he reached down, gently pulling the chemise that had settled at her waist the rest of the way over her body. This was his wife. The woman who would bear his children.

He wanted to see all of her. He wanted to worship all over her.

She allowed him to pull the chemise over her head, settling back on the bed with her head twisted to the side.

"Abby," he groaned, slowly lowering himself down once again. "Do you have any idea how gorgeous you are, my love?"

She looked at him then, her eyes questioning but soft even as he pressed into her, their bodies coming together in the most delicious way.

Her arms wrapped about him as she looked into his eyes. "Really?"

"Really. But I want you to know, when we're old and fat and—"

She laughed then, one of her legs hitching around his waist in a way that pushed the head of his cock into her soft, wet folds. He nearly forgot what he'd meant to say as sensation overwhelmed him.

Her lips found his and they kissed, long and deep, until he finally lifted up. "I will always love you."

Her gaze met his. "I will always love you too."

Slowly, he sank into her. She tensed and he stopped, waiting until she was ready once again. Slowly, carefully, he stretched her until she took all of him inside her body. Joined, he looked down into her eyes.

Abby was his. Forever.

Drawing out, he gently pushed back in, aware of her discomfort but also knowing that this was the beginning of the rest of their lives.

They went on like this, him moving with a carefulness that came from a deep desire not to hurt her even as his body cried for more.

And as she relaxed in his arms, he began to move more quickly, giving in to the ache that had built and built inside him.

Her hips began to rise to meet his until they were meeting like two parts of one body. The tension built in her again until she cried out, her insides tightening with such force around him that his own finish broke over him, pleasure crashing through him with his release.

They collapsed together in the middle of the bed, their bodies still twined together, where they stayed for several minutes.

His eyes grew heavy and the lack of sleep began to pull at his limbs. The bed was beyond comfortable and it was so perfect to have Abby tucked against his side like this.

Only her groan of discomfort pulled his eyes open again. "What's wrong?"

She gave him a soft smile. "I'm sore and I attempted to move."

He returned her grin, sliding out from under her and getting up to cross the room and pull the cord by the door. "What you need is a bath. And a snack."

She lifted her head to watch him, her naked body on full display as he walked back toward her.

She'd not be able to make love again, he knew that. But seeing her like that...

He peeled back the covers, pulling them over her body. She opened her arm, inviting him back in the bed. "That sounds wonderful, and then..."

"What?" he asked.

"A nap," she answered with an impish grin.

He slid under the covers as he snuggled her close. Some sleep sounded perfect to him.

CHAPTER SIXTEEN

ABBY WOKE as the sun set and she lifted her head to glance out the window to watch. The sky lit with oranges and pink, somehow mirroring the feelings in her heart.

She was glowing from within. Filled with joy at what today had brought. At last, she was home…here at Upton Falls with the man she loved. Rush.

She looked over at him, lying next to her, still asleep, his chest rising and falling. She grazed her fingertips over one of his biceps, and then traced over the thick muscles of his shoulder, running over his collarbone and down the center of his chest.

"Careful," he murmured, his eyes still closed. "You'll wake the beast."

A smile played at her lips. "Which beast is that?"

"The one who would keep you in this bed for days."

She laughed then, leaning over him as he wrapped an arm about her. Pulling her even closer, he lifted up to capture her mouth in a steamy kiss.

Her hands splayed out on his cheeks as she kissed him again. Staying in bed for days sounded like heaven.

A call from the yard sounded, muffled but she still heard it, and lifting her head, she looked out the window again.

The sun had sunk beneath the horizon but light still filled the sky, and she could make out two footmen standing at guard halfway down the drive. And beyond that, a lone horseman. She came to her knees, surprise and worry coursing through her.

She gasped, sitting up straighter as Rush bolted to a sitting position as well. One of his arms wrapped possessively around her waist.

"Blast," he rumbled as he turned to her. "Abby."

She looked down at him as he quickly kissed her mouth again.

"Stay here." And then he was up out of the bed, naked, crossing the room to look out the window before he turned back and began to dress.

She scrambled from the bed as well, grabbing her chemise. "I'll come with you."

With only his breeches on, he stopped and pulled her close again. "You'll stay here where you are safe. And if you hear anything, you hide."

"Hide?" she cried, holding on to his biceps. "Rush. What's happening?"

"I don't know yet, but I'm about to find out. Just promise me that you'll listen to what I've asked."

She gave a tentative nod, catching her lip as she continued to dress. There was little to be done with her hair, she didn't have time to pin it, but she plaited the thick mass in a loose braid, strands already escaping the front as she pulled on her dress and shoes. By the time she finished, Rush was already outside, making his way down the drive.

She caught her breath, watching out the windows but carefully remaining in the shadows. That was until she saw the rider.

It was Clarence.

Or who she now knew as Clarence. His real identity was still to be determined.

She stood for a moment, attempting to decide, and then she started down out of the room. She knew that Rush had told her to

114

stay, but if there were any questions left from these past months, Clarence was the man to answer them.

Roderick stood in the open door and she stopped behind him. He heard her anyway and looked over his shoulder. "My lady. You should return upstairs."

She shook her head. "That is my former guardian. Or the man I thought was my guardian."

Roderick's eyes widened and he gave her a quick gesture to remain hidden behind the door.

She did as he asked, not able to see but she could hear everything.

"What do you want, Westphal?" Rush called out, his voice booming over the front drive.

She heard Clarence's boots hit the ground, heavy and thick, his voice weaker. "I need to see Abigail."

"Not happening," Rush answered, iron behind his words.

But Clarence only sounded weak and tired. "I came to warn her."

"Warn her? About what?"

For a moment, Clarence was silent, and then he said, "So this is Upton Falls. It's pretty. Better than I imagined, truthfully."

Rush didn't respond for several seconds and so Clarence continued. "I'd like to sit. And mayhap trouble you for a glass of water."

"You'll get back on your horse and return to London," Rush growled out, "or I'll shoot you where you stand."

"You'd be doing me a favor, then," Clarence answered. "I won't make it back to London and if I did, they would finish the job they started. I'll be dead soon enough, but you're going to want to hear what I have to say."

Abby stepped out from behind the door then, in time to see Clarence pull back his coat, revealing a gaping wound in his chest near his shoulder, still oozing blood. Clarence's gaze caught hers and his eyes closed for a moment. "Please, Abigail. It's to your benefit that I'm here."

Rush's fist clenched as he gave a quick glance at her, before he turned back to Clarence. He didn't look at her as he spoke. "You were supposed to remain upstairs."

She slipped past Roderick and out onto the front steps, wrapping her arms about her middle. "I'd like to hear what he has to say."

Clarence took a tentative step away from his horse toward her as Rush lifted the pistol in his hand.

But Clarence hadn't made it a single step before he collapsed to the ground.

She clapped her hands to her mouth as Rush lurched forward.

He rustled through Clarence's clothing, and for a moment she didn't understand but then he pulled a pistol from Clarence's waistband and tossed it in the grass. She gasped as Rush continued his search, until he finally lifted Clarence from the ground to carry him inside.

———

IF SOMEONE HAD TOLD him that morning he'd be carrying Clarence Westphal, Rush would have never believed them.

But here he was…

The man was dying. He knew it. The wound was too large, the blood thick and still oozing, the man's skin waxy and void of color.

Had he really come here to give them information or was this some plot to hurt Abby one last time?

Rush would never let that happen.

He looked at Abby, still twenty yards away, as he jerked his chin. "He's still dangerous."

She gave a quick nod and slipped inside. He followed, walking through the door and turning in to the sitting room where he'd spent the previous night with Abby. Roderick carried in several blankets and laid them out on the settee before Rush set Clarence down.

From the corner of his eye, he noted that Abby hovered just beyond the doorway, not in the room but close enough to hear.

Rising, he grabbed the pitcher of water that sat on the buffet in the corner and poured the man a glass, bringing it back over to Clarence.

Lifting the man's head, Clarence's eyes slowly opened as he gratefully took a drink.

"Why don't we start with your real name?"

Clarence winced. "Figured that out, did you?"

He didn't answer as he waited. He gave Clarence, or whoever this man was, another drink before he lay his head back on the pillow.

"My name is Harvey Windborne." Harvey's eyes closed again. "And I was hired to impersonate Clarence Westphal."

"And the real Clarence?"

"I haven't a clue." The man shook his head. "My job was simple, though—marry Lady Abigail and sign the rights to Upton Falls over to the man who hired me. In exchange, I'd be a baron with all the rest of the land, money, and privileges that entailed."

Abby gasped.

"And who is the man who hired you?"

Harvey shook his head. "I don't know. But his solicitor is familiar to you, I believe. Guiltmore."

Rush's brows lifted. "Why would the man who hired you try to kill you?"

"You knew that Guiltmore was the one who attacked? How?"

"I have my ways."

"I don't know why the plan changed. Funny enough, they didn't explain before they shot me, but I can tell you that the same man who hired me is the one who is also attempting to buy your club."

His teeth gnashed together as his body went rigid. "Why the fuck would the man who tried to buy my club also be attacking Abby?"

Harvey shook his head. "He's collecting real estate. He did not share why or for whom with me." Harvey gave a weak cough as his head listed to one side. "But when I proved less than useful, he did not hesitate to dispose of me." And one of his hands lifted to indicate the wound. "You're still in grave danger and so is she."

Rush stared at Harvey for a moment as he tried to process all that he'd just heard. This wasn't just a man attempting to buy some clubs. He'd set up an impostor to steal the barony. That took serious connections. And he had an eye for far more than a few illegal businesses in London. Rush glanced back at his wife again, her hands covering her mouth as tears shone in her eyes.

Rising, he gestured to Roderick. "This man is still dangerous. Have him relocated upstairs but have a footman guard the hall. Fetch the doctor and see that he's given any water or food that he requires."

"I'm sorry," Harvey said.

Rush looked back to see his eyes open again, but he didn't look at Rush, instead his gaze was fixed on Abby.

"For what I did to you. I'm sorry."

She gave the barest nod. Leaving Harvey, Rush exited the room, catching Abby up in his arms as the first tear fell onto her cheek. Holding her tightly, he buried her head in his chest.

"Rush," she cried into his shoulder. "I thought this business was behind us but it's just beginning, isn't it?"

But he shook his head. "Sweetheart. I told you, I'll not allow anyone to hurt you. This is our home and now that we're married, it's beyond their reach. Whoever they are."

She gave a tentative nod but Rush knew in part she was right.

This was just beginning.

And it was time he and his brothers became more serious about facing this threat. They were going to war. But he'd learned one valuable fact throughout this entire affair.

And that was in this, he could count on his brothers absolutely.

They were a family.

And they would surely help him keep Abby safe.

He held her tighter as her arms wrapped about his waist. "I love you," she whispered into his shoulder. "So much."

"I love you too," he said into her hair. "Forever. You are my future, Abigail Smith, and I'll see you cared for no matter what comes to pass. I promise."

She looked at him then, her head tipping back as her lips parted, the barest smile pulling at them. "I trust you with everything. All that I am and all that I have."

He kissed her then, long and deep and full of the promises he intended to keep.

EPILOGUE

ONE MONTH LATER...

RUSH STOOD on the front lawn, his chest wide as he waited. Tris was arriving today and he'd be lying to himself if he didn't confess that he was excited to show his brother his new home. His new life.

He'd spent the past fortnight of his marriage sending a great many letters. To his eldest brother, Ace, to Tris, Gris, and Fulton, to Upton, and Easton.

And they'd begun to formulate a plan.

Tris was to come here to help make certain that Abby was safe. Fulton would keep up his trade, but Gris would stop the production of his gin temporarily to keep the club going. It was making all of them rich, and much as Rush knew that Abby's estate provided for them, he'd help ensure their future by maintaining both the estate and the club.

But he loved Upton Falls already. It was everything he'd dreamed his life might be. He spent much of the mornings riding the grounds and getting a feel for the crops and the animals. In the afternoons, he worked on the books for both the club and the estate.

And in the evenings…well, he did have a new wife. The evenings were the best part of the day by far, except, of course, for the nights.

He smiled to himself even as Tris came into view.

On horseback, Rush recognized Tris instantly. Large and imposing, he looked even more so atop a massive shire. The animal was tall and muscular with thick legs, his glossy black coat shining in the sun.

Tris sat atop him with a straight back and the sort of easy swagger that told Rush his brother had made a full recovery.

"This is your home?" Tris boomed out as he rode closer.

Rush spread out his arms. "Like it?"

Tris's eyes scanned the grounds. "So many trees." He sounded skeptical.

Which made Rush laugh. "You can ride for miles and miles and not run into a soul."

"And you like that?" Tris asked, finally reaching him and swinging down from his horse.

"I love it."

Tris clapped his back. "Well, good for you, brother." Then he grimaced, rolling his arm. Did the injury pain him still?

Rush would ask him once they were settled inside. Instead, he gave a nod of thanks. "Thank you. I wish the wedding might have been different. I want the rest of our family to meet my bride."

Tris looked to the house, studying the stately farm. "They will. But let's work on keeping everyone safe first, shall we?"

"Sounds good. Thank you, Tris."

They started up the drive just as a carriage appeared on the road.

Rush tensed, wondering who else would be coming. The carriage was ornate, with red accents and inlaid gold.

Tris turned too, his massive chest expanding as he watched the carriage ramble toward them, the team of dapples perfectly matched as they pranced down the drive.

The carriage stopped just before them, a footman hoping down to open the carriage door.

But from the moment a slippered foot appeared, Rush's brows drew together in confusion.

And that confusion only grew as a beautiful young woman appeared, with auburn hair and flashing green eyes, a smile playing about her lips as she looked at them both.

"What a reception." She laughed, as Rush recovered himself and stepped forward.

"Forgive me, I wasn't expecting guests, other than my brother here." And then he gave a quick bow. "I am Lord Smith and this is my brother, Lord Triston. Welcome to Upton Falls."

She curtsied to both of them as her companion was handed out of the carriage. "Lady Emma Blake. Pleased to make your acquaintance."

"To what do we owe the pleasure, Lady Emma?" Tris sounded anything but pleased. His voice dripped with derision as he gave a menacing scowl.

Still, Rush gave a quick breath of relief to know that his brother had at least gotten her address correct. He was certain this was some neighbor and he'd like to make a decent first impression. His suspicion was confirmed a moment later. "I live on the neighboring property. I was hoping to visit with the lady of the house, though I am aware that I come uninvited. Forgive me. We're more relaxed here than in Town."

Rush waved his hand. "No need to apologize. I shall find Lady Smith for you."

"Wonderful," she cried as Rush offered her his arm. But he noted that her gaze lingered on Tris...the breadth of his chest, the cut of his jaw.

He ought to tell her not to bother, Tris was as likely to fall for a country miss as the sun was to set in the east. A gritty Londoner to his core, Tris hadn't dallied with a proper lady for some time. Not since the last one's husband had attempted to kill him. And before that, he'd had some run-in with a debutante's father...

But he kept his thoughts to himself as Tris gave the woman a fierce scowl. His brother would surely send the message without Rush's intervention.

But to his surprise, Miss Emma didn't appear intimidated by the scowl. Rather, she gave Tris an even larger smile as she looked back at his horse. "Beautiful animal."

"Ornery as the day is long," he grunted, crossing his arms as his grimace deepened. But Emma only shrugged as Rush began to lead her toward the house.

"Funny thing about the days," she countered. "They're getting shorter. 'Tis the season."

Tris snorted. "You're a clever one."

Emma didn't answer as she looked at Rush instead. "We're having our annual autumn soirée this Friday and while I will give all the details to your wife, know that you and your guest are most welcome."

He heard Tris groan. And he knew that Tris was here to do him a favor, but the brother in him couldn't help but answer. "Lady Emma, we'd be most delighted to attend. All of us."

OH DEAR. *Tris and Emma don't seem to like each other very much! Want to see if those sparks are love or hate?* **"A Score with a Scoundrel"** *is next in the* Lords of Temptation *series!*

A SCORE WITH A SCOUNDREL

TAMMY ANDRESEN

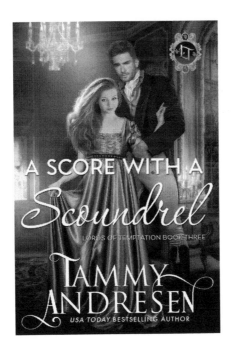

Miss Emma Blake tapped her toe beneath her skirts as she and her mother greeted an endless line of guests.

The autumn soiree was an event her family held every year and her mother had determined that they'd do so again despite the less-than-ideal circumstances. Emma had more or less agreed, though now that she was here, she found she could not decide if she wished to race recklessly from this receiving line and into the ballroom where the music had already begun or if she wanted to run up to her room and hide beneath the covers of her bed.

Every detail appeared the same as previous soirees with red-and-gold garland and wreaths adorning every mantel, doorway, and chandelier. And though candles filled the entry, hall, and ballroom while a ten-piece orchestra was stationed at one end, this year was not the same.

Not at all. And not ever again.

Because next to her mother, where her father should have stood, was a blank space.

"Keep your smile firmly in place," her mother whispered from her spot next to Emma. "You must appear the perfect hostess."

Perfect. The word had been bandied about so often of late, Emma wondered if it had lost its meaning. No one was perfect.

Least of all her. But suddenly the expectation was there. A perfect lady would marry the best lord. That was what her mother repeated over and over until Emma wished to go mad from the repetition. Granted, she was considered attractive by many. She was tall, curvy, with striking auburn hair and green eyes. But she was far from a successful debutante. Her season in London had been going well enough until her father's illness had cut it short. Though she was not as demure as many would like, the gentlemen, at least, had seemed to like her bolder nature. Though her mother had sworn that very trait would lead to ruin.

Emma's uncle appeared, Emma's younger sister, Natalie, on his arm and she gave herself a bit of a shake as she watched them approach. Her uncle looked so much like her father that Emma ached a bit to every time she shared his company. She and her father had always been close. Where Emma and her mother so often disagreed, her father had simply loved his daughter. She missed him so much, the pain of his loss sometimes threatened to engulf her.

Her uncle had become the new Viscount Northville but he'd been kind enough to leave their mother, Emma, and Natalie in their home while they first grieved and then decided upon their future.

Though the only decision left seemed to be whom Emma would marry. Her mother had some inheritance, much of her dowry remained, and her father had left a small property for his wife, but it was, in every way, far less grand than the ancestral home of the Viscount Northville. Which meant that it was left to Emma to marry well and keep her mother in the life to which they'd become accustomed.

Emma shook her head. No one had asked her if she wished to marry, or if she cared about how large her future home would be. She didn't...on either account.

What she wanted was some measure of freedom. The ability to find herself and a future that made her feel satisfied rather than forever restless. She was certain a husband would be the opposite experience.

Her mother gave a glittering smile to the Earl of Berwick and his son, the Viscount Marsden, the next guests in line. "So wonderful to see you both," her mother laughed, the tinkling sound ringing out like a bell. "It's been ages." Then she waved airily toward Emma. "You remember my daughter, Miss Blake."

Berwick leaned in to take her mother's hands, raising one to his lips as his son stopped in front of her, giving a short bow. "Lady Emma. You've grown up since last I saw you." His gaze raked over her in a way that made her wildly uncomfortable.

"And you, my lord, look exactly the same." It wasn't exactly true. Was he ten years her senior? He'd filled out a great deal, mostly in the middle and his hair had thinned considerably. Still, he wasn't entirely unfortunate to look upon and he would be an earl. Her mother would surely consider him an excellent catch.

She caught her mother's approving look out of the corner of her eye as Marsden leaned forward to whisper into her ear. "You must save me a dance."

She gave a nod of acceptance as he moved closer still. Emma

resisted the urge to step back, realizing that she'd answered her earlier question about which way she'd like to run. She no longer had any desire go into the ballroom, she now wished to go directly to her room.

But she kept her feet planted and the father and son moved on, making way for the next guests.

She didn't look at them, her eyelids had fluttered closed as she attempted to calm the beat of her heart, the desire to run. She'd like to be on her horse, riding over the open fields. Or perhaps in London, blending into the sea of people. Anywhere but here.

"Why hello," her mother gushed from next to her. "Such a pleasure to finally meet you."

Emma's eyes snapped back open, her breath catching as her gaze collided with another's.

Lord Triston Smith. Her heartbeat increased, pounding in her chest as his dark eyes held hers captive. Near black in color, they were fringed with long lashes, which managed to draw even more attention to his glittering gaze. Those lashes were the only soft thing about him. That and his waving dark hair.

Every other part of him was hard from his jaw to the chiseled cut of his shoulders, right down to his powerful thighs on full display in the tight breeches he wore.

His mouth was set in a perpetually hard frown, at least that was her impression. This was only the second time she'd met him, the first encounter being very brief, but his mouth appeared natural in the stern expression.

Which should likely have frightened her.

But somehow, it wasn't fear but sizzling awareness and a keen interest that coursed through her once again. Why had the handful of words they'd exchanged been as gruff as his stern frown? Was there any softness underneath that hard exterior?

She shivered, not with fear but with interest as his brother, Lord Smith, took her mother's offered hand.

His wife came next. Lady Smith was as sweet as her looks implied.

During their one meeting, the beautiful blonde had been warm and generous with her time and her compliments.

Emma had instantly liked her.

"Lady Emma," Lady Smith gave her a large smile. "So good to see you again. Thank you for having us."

"I'm so glad you've come." Those felt like the first genuine words she'd said all evening. And something inside her uncoiled, her entire body relaxing. "I've been hoping to come see you again, but we've been so busy with preparations."

Lady Smith waved her hand. "I understand. Perhaps this week coming we could have tea."

"I'd like that very much," she answered even as she watched Lord Triston greet her mother. He bowed, that stiff frown still marking his face, hardly uttering a word beyond a gruff, "Good evening."

Even her mother eyed him with a bit of skepticism as she quickly replied. "Good evening."

Lord Triston was the exact sort of man her mother would despise. And not just because he was rougher in every way from a normal lord. He was a third son, unlikely to ever gain a title. That was his worst sin of all.

Emma attempted to care. She really did. She knew how important a good marriage was to her mother. But as he looked into those dark eyes, excitement settled deep in the pit of her stomach.

"Lord Triston," Emma supplied with a shaking breath. "A pleasure to see you again."

And she meant to words. Far more than she ought.

———

Tris groaned to himself as he stared into the green eyes that he was certain belonged to the devil.

Oh, Lady Emma looked innocent enough.

Auburn hair and ivory skin. Full, lush pink lips that always had a ready smile. And he wouldn't even start on her figure. Because that is where the devilment began. Her curves were made for sin.

And the look in her eyes… They were the color of grass after a spring rain and the tiny yellow flecks appeared like sunshine itself ,but beneath that…

They held the glint of trouble.

He'd recognize the look anywhere.

He was one of five brothers who'd grown up as the bastard sons of the Earl of Easton. Through a stroke of fate, and the helping hand of their one legitimate sibling, they had been legitimatized, but they'd been raised on the East End of London. And one learned to spot bad intentions with a single glance and this lady may as well be holding up a sign.

Is she did, it would read…

I'll ruin your life if you let me.

Though a lord now, Tris had never actually expected to be so. After spending much of his childhood thieving, fighting, and generally causing mayhem, he'd settled into the sport of boxing as a way to channel his feelings and his need for chaos.

The anger that had plagued him still simmered underneath the surface. He'd just learned to focus those feelings into his training and into his fights.

Fairly certain he was too explosive for *any* woman, he knew without a doubt that a woman like Lady Emma was as far away as the moon.

He saw the interest shining in her eyes. He'd seen it before. Ladies liked his strength, they found his hard edges intriguing, until they brushed against one.

Once she was married, she might invite him into her bed for a torrid affair and he'd likely accept. The attraction he felt for her was near explosive, so deep it was a well that would surely drown him.

But as a debutante, he'd best stay as far away from her as possible. He had his own goals and dallying with a daughter of a powerful family was the surest way to see them crushed.

Which is why, when he stopped in front of her, he looked over her left shoulder, not meeting her gaze, as he murmured, "Lady Emma."

"My lord," she replied, her breath catching on the second word. Despite his best efforts, he tensed at the breathiness he heard. Her obvious interest.

He willed himself back to calm, knowing that here, of all places, he could not lose control of himself. He already stuck out at this ball or party or whatever the hell they'd called the bloody affair.

Taller, larger than every man, and far more muscled, he barely fit into his coat. The rest of these titled gentlemen had a softness about them. Easy lives, good food. He bet none of them had ever brawled in the streets or had knife fights with boys twice their size. They'd never fought to feed their baby sisters or thieved for the same reason.

Tris had always been filled with raw aggression and it didn't fit in this clean and beautiful world. He looked about the entry with its soaring ceilings and intricate plaster. The polish of the carved banister shone in the candlelight as guests made their way up the curved stairs to the ballroom.

"Thank you for coming," Emma continued, leaning forward in a way that better displayed her cleavage. He couldn't help himself. He looked down at the plump, round, smooth flesh.

His cock gave a definite twitch as he forced himself not to notice how her bosom was precisely the perfect amount. Not over much, it was just enough, assuring him that her tits would fill a man's hands. He tried to tear his gaze away but failed miserably.

Nor could he help but trace the narrow curve of her waist or the flair of her hips with his gaze. He'd bet her ass was nice and plump and round.

He clenched both fists at his sides. "The pleasure is mine." The words sat bitter on his tongue. It was not a pleasure but a torture.

"Will you be staying at Upton Falls for long?"

The answer was that he didn't know. The family ran a gaming hell, Hell's Corner. When a competitor had threatened his brother's wife, Tris had agreed to come here to ensure her safety.

But damned if he was telling this woman any of that. He knew she only asked because she was making plans…what sort he couldn't say. But whatever they were, he wanted no part of them. "Not long."

She gave him an overly bright smile that told him of her disappointment. For his part, he'd stay at this particular party for as short a time as possible and then he'd slip away. Lady Emma's home was the neighboring house to his brother's. He could walk back at any point. In fact, the night air would likely help cool his overheated skin.

Saying a curt goodbye, he followed his brother Rush and Rush's wife Abby up the grand stairs and into the ballroom, his teeth grinding together as he noted the marble floors that gleamed under his feet.

Next to him, some woman with plumes of feathers sticking out her headdress gave an overly enthusiastic giggle. "I just love the Northvilles' Soiree. What shall we do when they no longer host it?"

A sneer pulled at his lip. The carpets were thick and lush, a red that only accented the decorations for the soiree. Christ, even that word spoke of snobbery.

Soiree.

Soiree.

It sounded odder each time he repeated it. Utter shit. A sea of sparkling women passed him, all in jewels that caught the candlelight and twinkled as their wearers moved.

One of those stones could have fed an entire tenement house where he came from. Where people were packed in like fish in a barrel and still starving.

He tugged on the lapels of his jacket. What was he even doing here?

He'd wanted no part of this life. He'd keep his brother safe. And Abby too. The woman was as sweet as they came, but he'd never wished to attend a soiree.

He already had a profession as a boxer and that suited him perfectly well. The only reason he'd agreed to help his family with the club was that he wanted to take his career further.

At nearly thirty, he was growing too old for the ring. It had occurred to him that he might start of a boxing club of his own. He could train and spar and use the club as the release of pressure without so much risk to his personal health.

Which was why he'd entered into the gaming business with his brothers. Because while it created one headache after another, it also afforded him enough income that he'd nearly saved all that he needed for the purchase of his own club.

And leaving to help Rush in the country would only prove to his brothers that they could run the business without him.

A good plan, if he did say so himself, except for this one complication. He'd landed himself at a bloody soiree.

Stationing himself against a wall, he leaned back, crossing his ankles and his arms in an attempt to make himself as unappealing as possible.

It didn't work. Woman after woman eyed him over her fan, eyes filled with interest or suggestion or both.

He ignored any implied invitations.

A few years back, he'd dallied with a countess. When her husband had found out, Triston nearly landed in the tower. He'd only avoided it by hopping on a ship with his brother Fulton and spending three months in Italy while his brother ran wine.

He'd not make such a mistake again.

Besides, any desire he might feel for these women was dulled but his dislike for their vapid self-regard.

Lady Emma entered the ballroom, her hand tucked into some man's arm. She laughed as he spoke, her smile so large, it looked brittle.

He was the exact sort that Tris despised. Soft. That was the word for it.

With a growl of disgust, he pushed off the wall and went in search of Rush. He was leaving. His brother could spend as long as he wished but Tris had had enough.

Preorder **A Score with a Scoundrel** *today!*

Keep up with all the latest news, sales, freebies, and releases by joining my newsletter!

www.tammyandresen.com

Hugs!

ABOUT THE AUTHOR

Tammy Andresen lives with her husband and three children just outside of Boston, Massachusetts. She grew up on the Seacoast of Maine, where she spent countless days dreaming up stories in blueberry fields and among the scrub pines that line the coast. Her mother loved to spin a yarn and Tammy filled many hours listening to her mother retell the classics. It was inevitable that at the age of eighteen, she headed off to Simmons College, where she studied English literature and education. She never left Massachusetts but some of her heart still resides in Maine and her family visits often.

Find out more about Tammy:
http://www.tammyandresen.com/
https://www.facebook.com/authortammyandresen
https://twitter.com/TammyAndresen
https://www.pinterest.com/tammy_andresen/
https://plus.google.com/+TammyAndresen/

OTHER TITLES BY TAMMY

Lords of Scandal

Duke of Daring

Marquess of Malice

Earl of Exile

Viscount of Vice

Baron of Bad

Earl of Sin

_____

Earl of Gold

Earl of Baxter

Duke of Decandence

Marquess of Menace

Duke of Dishonor

Baron of Blasphemy

Viscount of Vanity

Earl of Infamy

Laird of Longing

_____

Duke of Chance

Marquess of Diamonds

Queen of Hearts

Baron of Clubs

Earl of Spades

King of Thieves

Marquess of Fortune

Calling All Rakes

Wanted: An Earl for Hire

Needed: A Dishonorable Duke

Found: Bare with a Baron

Vacancy: Viscount Required

Lost: The Love of a Lord

Missing: An Elusive Marquess

Wanted: Title of Countess

The Dark Duke's Legacy

Her Wicked White

Her Willful White

His Wallflower White

Her Wanton White

Her Wild White

His White Wager

Her White Wedding

The Rake's Ruin

When only an Indecent Duke Will Do

How to Catch an Elusive Earl

Where to Woo a Bawdy Baron

When a Marauding Marquess is Best

What a Vulgar Viscount Needs

Who Wants a Brawling Baron

When to Dare a Dishonorable Duke

The Wicked Wallflowers

Earl of Dryden

Too Wicked to Woo

Too Wicked to Wed

Too Wicked to Want

How to Reform a Rake

Don't Tell a Duke You Love Him

Meddle in a Marquess's Affairs

Never Trust an Errant Earl

Never Kiss an Earl at Midnight

Make a Viscount Beg

Wicked Lords of London

Earl of Sussex

My Duke's Seduction

My Duke's Deception

My Earl's Entrapment

My Duke's Desire

My Wicked Earl

Brethren of Stone

The Duke's Scottish Lass

Scottish Devil

Wicked Laird

Kilted Sin

Rogue Scot

The Fate of a Highland Rake

A Laird to Love

Christmastide with my Captain

My Enemy, My Earl

Heart of a Highlander

A Scot's Surrender

A Laird's Seduction

Taming the Duke's Heart

Taming a Duke's Reckless Heart

Taming a Duke's Wild Rose

Taming a Laird's Wild Lady

Taming a Rake into a Lord

Taming a Savage Gentleman

Taming a Rogue Earl

Fairfield Fairy Tales

Stealing a Lady's Heart

Hunting for a Lady's Heart

Entrapping a Lord's Love: Coming in February of 2018

American Historical Romance

Lily in Bloom

Midnight Magic

The Golden Rules of Love

Boxsets!!

Taming the Duke's Heart Books 1-3

American Brides

A Laird to Love

Wicked Lords of London

Manufactured by Amazon.ca
Bolton, ON